"FORWARD, CHARGE!"

At Major Harding's command the twenty Lightning troopers spurred their horses through the brush and woods along the side of the stream. Two hundred yards below they found a dozen Comanches trying to shoot the horses they had stolen. Six were down already. The riflemen used their long guns and knocked two redmen off their ponies, and scattered the rest.

From the side, thirty Comanches stormed in to attack Major Harding. Just at that time the other twenty Lightning troopers under Lieutenant Petroff burst out of the woods from downstream and sent a volley into the charging Comanches. Five fell dead before they could turn and swarm to the left, away from the river.

They rode hard, leaving their prize, leaving their dead, intent only on getting away with their lives.

Also in the PONY SOLDIERS series:

#1: SLAUGHTER AT BUFFALO CREEK
#2: COMANCHE MASSACRE

COMANCHE MOON

Chet Cunningham

LEISURE BOOKS NEW YORK CITY

A LEISURE BOOK

Published by

Dorchester Publishing Co., Inc.
6 East 39th Street
New York, NY 10016

Printed in the United States of America

COMANCHE MOON

1

A dry, eerie wind whipped around them; the September sun bore down unrelentingly on the seven blue uniformed men huddled in desperation behind the only cover they had: a twenty-four inch deep dry wash in the Texas high plains. At least they were backed up against a thirty-foot high crumbling granite cliff, giving them protection to the rear.

A rifle snarled in front of them and a chunk of hot lead zinged a foot over the top of their protective dirt wall and splattered into the cliff.

"Lieutenant, how in Christ's name we gonna get out of here?" a trooper called, his voice a pleading wail.

Lieutenant Dan Edwards took off his light brown campaign hat and wiped sweat from his forehead. He had no answer for the private in B Company of the Second Cavalry, no answer at all.

His hand came back from his forehead with blood on it. A graze. He looked at the six men with him. The Comanche attack had been a total surprise. His patrol tried to ride away but the warriors had them surrounded. They dismounted and found the best cover available. Then, in a slashing attack, the Comanches drove off their horses.

Lieutenant Edwards figured they had enough ammunition to hold out until it was dark. Then they could slip away. Maybe.

He watched over the lip of the small dirt bank. Two hundred yards ahead was a slight rise in the endless Texas plains. Behind that protection were forty Comanche warriors eager to take scalps.

Nearly half of them were armed with rifles, but none of those were repeating Spencers, thank God. To the left lay an open area a hundred yards wide. Not a chance to outrun the Comanche bullets that way. To the right the little water course flattened out for another two hundred yards before it gave out entirely in a sweeping half mile of unbroken prairie.

Lieutenant Edwards still had no idea where the hostiles had come from. One moment his detail was on a boring, routine scouting patrol to see if there were any Indian activity out twenty miles from Fort Comfort.

The next moment they were under attack by a howling mass of Comanche who skillfully boxed them in and drove them backward against this bluff and sealed off both exits. For being notorious for individual action, this band of savages had worked extremely well together. Their tactics were perfect: surprise, containment . . . eventual victory.

"Come on, Lieutenant, we got to do something," a trooper with a bloody kerchief around his left arm said. "Maybe if we all jumped up and charged the bastards . . . ."

"Shut up, Murdock," Corporal Lawson said. "The lieutenant is figuring it out right now."

Lieutenant Edwards swallowed. That was the trouble, there wasn't a damn thing left to figure out. The Comanches had eliminated any possible avenue of escape by luck or design, it didn't matter now.

A volley of six shots slammed into the top of the dirt wall showering them with alkaline dust.

"We wait them out until darkness," Lieutenant Edwards said with more confidence than he felt. "Let's have a casualty report. How's Greggson?"

"Real bad, Lieutenant," Corporal Lawson said. "Took one through the lung. He can't move or he dies. Outside of that we got some scratches. Rest of us are able to make a good account of ourselves."

The troopers pressed against the rough face of the low wall. Their army regulation, knee-high brown leather boots showed spurs on the heels, useless now. Most of the blue pants were dirt smeared. The cartridge belts still held half the issue of rifle rounds and supported a regulation, leather holstered Amy issue .44 revolver. The men's dark blue shirts were sweat stained, sticking to their skin. A swarm of small gnats and stinging flies pestered them into constant slapping and waving.

Lieutenant Edwards took another quick look over the top of the wash from a different spot. Nothing. The hostiles were waiting. What for? Like most of the Comanches, this band had a smart leader. He knew they had a sure victory here and he evidently didn't want to rush things or risk his warriors. Thirst alone would defeat the troopers if the day became hot enough.

It sneaked out of the clear blue sky with only a whisper, then a "thonking" sound as a Comanche war arrow buried itself six inches deep in the soft dirt.

"Damnit!" Lieutenant Edwards brayed. "That's one way we can't defend ourselves. Spread out along the wall as much as possible and lay on your sides. That was probably a marker."

As he spoke three more arrows shot high into the sky and then dropping like mortar shells, sliced into the ground just in front of the wall.

"Rifles up, and over the wall. Keep your head down. On my signal fire two rounds each." When the weapons were in place he said: "Now!"

The six Spencers scattered twelve rounds into and over the Indians' protection.

Thirty seconds later twenty arrows dropped silently out of the sky. Corporal Lawson screamed in pain. One of the Comanche arrows tore into his thigh. The complete arrowhead and its backward prongs were buried in his flesh. He reached down and broke off the shaft, blanching white as he did so, and shaking his head to keep from passing out.

Nobody else was hit.

"Another round," Lieuteant Edwards ordered. Five rifles fired this time.

A horse charged over the protective hill from the left side. It must have a rider on it, but all they saw was a rawhide band around the pony and one foot locked under it. The Comanche rode on the far side of the horse in safety.

They waited. It was a taunt. The rider got within a hundred yards, gave a furious Comanche war cry, then wheeled and rode back, now on the other side of the mount still almost out of sight.

They waited. Another flight of arrows came in but missed them. Again a rider bolted from the protection of the hill and rode toward them. Lieutenant Edwards lifted up, saw the rider and pushed his rifle over the top of the dirt. Then he lifted up and fired three times, as fast as he could lever the Spencer. The pony went down, dead as he hit the ground and rolled. Two rifle rounds from the hill answered, spraying dirt on Edwards.

He moved, lifted up and sent two more shots at the Comanche warrior who had kicked free of the horse and now ran for the hill. Edwards brought him down with his second shot just as the officer bellowed in pain and jolted away from the two foot dirt wall.

A rifle round from the enemy had smashed his left shoulder.

Two troopers pulled him back into the protection of the wall and a moment later the arrows began to drop in on them again. At least fifty of them fell in the first wave, Edwards figured. He held his bleeding shoulder. One goddamned Comanche for seven U.S. troopers. A damn poor exchange.

Edwards thought about his wife, Olive, and his little boy, Will, just four, and Martha who was over six. He realized that he would never see them again. There was no way out of this trap.

He shook his head, refusing to accept his own logic. There had to be a way out. He eyed the jumble of rocks to the left. It was almost a hundred yards. They could move and fire, move and fire. That was better than laying here and getting picked off like fish in a barrel.

"Men, I'm sorry I got you in this mess. I still don't know where that bunch came from. This decision is up to you. Should we lay here and get slaughtered like sheep, or should we see if we can get to the outcropping over there?"

"A hundred yards?" Corporal Lawson asked.

"About. We'll move and fire, spaced five yards apart, run, drop and fire at the hill, get up and run again. Fifteen twenty yards at a bite. Zig-zagging wouldn't hurt. All right men, what do you say?"

All six of them nodded. Greggson was barely conscious. He pulled his six-gun, cocked the hammer and gave his rifle to Murdock.

"Get the hell out of here," Greggson said, a smile on his rugged face.

"All right, up on your feet, but squat down. We all go at once and string out. Fire while running might be better. If you stop they'll have an easier target. We might surprise them. Ready?"

Edwards looked at the men. It was his fault. He should have had some outriders. Damn!

"Let's go!"

He had forgotten about his shattered left shoulder. He led the group. He held the Spencer with his right hand but could only steady it with his left as he fired a shot at the bank. He kept running and almost dropped the weapon as he levered in a new round.

Ten yards! He saw out of the corner of his eye the other men stringing out. Two troopers passed him, firing as they ran. Lawson limped badly on his wounded leg and fell behind.

For ten seconds there was no firing from the hill. Then it came, a dozen rounds. Lawson went down first. He took a round in the chest and spilled over sideways and never moved.

Ahead the others kept running. Murdock was in

front. A dozen rounds slammed into the dirt around him but missed. They had covered fifty yards, then Gonzales caught a round in the side. It rammed into his heart and he flopped on the prairie.

Another twenty seconds. Edwards told himself as his feet pounded on the ground. He wasn't used to running. A chunk of hot lead caught his pants leg and zapped through. No damage. He was almost there.

He heard a scream from behind him. Six Comanches rode out on their ponies waving fourteen-foot long lances. Edwards wanted to stop and aim and kill one of the bastards, but if he did he would be a perfect target for the riflemen still firing.

He never felt the bullet strike. His left leg broke under him as he stepped down and another slug hit him in the chest. Fewer targets for them. Damn!

He plowed a furrow in the ground and lay there in the dirt and sand without moving. He could play dead. Yes. But the Comanches mutilated their enemies. He tried to stand but fell.

His rifle lay beyond reach. He grabbed at his six-gun, but it also had spilled out of its holster.

Edwards saw Murdock reach the first rock, but before he could dive behind it two rounds took him in the chest and he flopped back lifelessly.

Private Smith dropped beside him.

"Let me help you, Lieutenant!"

The words were barely from his mouth when his face exploded as a rifle round entered from behind his ear and came out his eye, taking half the face with it.

He fell over Edwards. The cavalry officer pushed

the body away and grabbed Smith's revolver, then began to crawl toward the rocks. The rifle firing from the small hill had stopped. Edwards gritted his teeth, fought down the jolting, searing pain and crawled, dragged his useless leg behind him.

His eyes misted as sand blew in them. When he cleared them he saw the six Indian mounts. The riders had drawn up three on each side of him. They walked their horses as he crawled. He lifted the revolver to fire at them but a lance swung down and smashed into his wrist breaking the bones, dumping the pistol out of reach.

The warriors watched him, curious how far he could go.

Edwards was damned if he would stop. He'd make the rocks if it was the last thing he did. He pulled himself with his right elbow, levering himself forward, his left arm not functioning at all. For five minutes he worked his way over the grass and dirt, then he could move no farther. He made one more lunge over the hot dirt and sand and grass and fell on his face. Slowly he rolled over on his back.

For a moment, for an eternity, for ever and ever he saw the glinting white eye provided metal point of the lance poise over his chest. Then so slowly that he could count the years between the ticks of a watch, the glistening, razor-like edge of the point came toward his chest. It took an eternity to lower the three feet from where the Comanche held it.

Or did it come in the blink of an eyelid?

Lieutenant Dan Edwards would never be sure.

He felt the melting hot point of the lance tip as it penetrated the skin on his chest over his heart. Then the world spun and the Indians merged and their scream of triumph boiled into his mind. The Comanches shrilled and laughed as a sharp knife cut a deep line across his forehead and an Indian grabbed his hair and began to pull.

Then the lance drove deeper as a crushing load hit his chest and smashed him miles into the earth until he was sure he was at the very center of the planet. But before he could see what was there, an oily black cloud closed around everything and the darkness was total, unequivocally and forever and forever.

Above the body of Lieutenant Edwards, the leader of the Comanches grunted in admiration. The white eye had been a true warrior. He had led his men in one last desperate attempt to escape.

Walking White Eagle admired those qualities in any man, white or Indian, even in the hated People Eaters, the Tonkawa. White Eagle withdrew his lance from the body and stepped down from Flying Wind, his new war horse that had matured during the past few months.

There had been seven of the Pony Soldiers. He had not wanted to attack anyone this close to the fort of Captain Two Guns, but there had been no choice. Just over the next rise were the two hundred horses the raiding party had captured in Mexico. Also there waited the five children and the three women they brought back. The Pony Soldiers would have seen them.

He watched as the warriors claimed their coup, took the scalps and argued over whose bullet had killed which man. There would be much for the council to decide later. The bodies were stripped of their clothes. The boot tops were especially prized by the Indian women to cut off and make items for wearing. The pistols and rifles were gathered up, as well as the spare ammunition from the strange surcingles the troopers wore.

Already they had captured the horses, discarded the heavy saddles, but kept the bridles. The army blankets would be saved. Soon the warriors had taken the scalps, then ceremonially slashed the bodies so the white Pony Soldiers would not be able to fight them again in the hereafter. It was always done when there was time.

They loaded the one man in their party who had died on his war pony. He would be buried the next day on the highest point they could find. It was too far to take him back to the summer camp for burial.

White Eagle gave a signal and the warriors rode to where they had left the horses and captives. Now they would have to ride faster and longer, to be sure that they could be far away when the Pony Soldiers found the remains of their patrol. Captain Two Guns would be angry.

At the herd, they checked to be sure the women and five children were all tied securely on horses, then they rode out, driving the animals ahead of them, setting a swift pace, the canter, the pace that a horse can use for hour after hour with little wear and tear on its body. Indian ponies could canter all day and cover more than six and a half miles an hour.

On a good day they could move a hundred miles without stopping. The stolen horses were not grass fed, nor as lean and sturdy as the Indian ponies. They could make no more than fifty miles before needing a rest.

White Eagle was an expert on horses. He knew it

did no good to go on a long raid into Mexico to steal horses only to have them driven to death on the way back to the campsite.

The three women captives were young and sturdy, they would have many babies. The children were all four and five years old and would adapt well to the Comanche way of life and grow up as members of the people and, at the same time, inject fresh blood into the band. Just like a herd of horses, there had to be fresh blood brought in from time to time to prevent the father-daughter breeding that would provide unhealthy children.

After two days of hard riding, the White Eagle band warriors eased off, and camped early one night. The owners of the three women slaves stripped them naked and paraded them around the camp, showing off their beauty. One warrior traded his woman captive for ten horses. He had three wives at home, but he was short of horses.

It took them three more days to come to the White River and where it slashed upward through the great cap rock that guarded the approaches to what everyone called the Staked Plains.

White Eagle had changed plans for wintering a month ago. When two more bands of Comanche had moved into the Staked Plains for the winter where they would be sure that the white eye Pony Soldiers would not seek them out. Pony Soldiers had never ventured onto the high plateau in the western panhandle of Texas.

Now they moved the captured horses into the narrow ravine of the White River and drove them upward. The river cut a gorge, but soon it raised quickly through rapids and small falls. At each point there had been a usable trail cut round the falls and over the rapids, so the stream had actually carved out a stairway up the eight hundred feet to the top of the tall escarpment.

Few knew of this trail, and the Comanches would share it with no one. At last they made it to the top with the captives and horses and the whole camp turned out in welcome for the returning warriors and their booty.

The dancing that night was wild and exciting. The warriors rode into the council fire, each flung his lance into the buffalo robe in front of the council, and gave a glowing and heroic account of his own cunning and bravery in the raid and in fighting the terrible Pony Soldiers.

After the claims were all made, the council members moved close together to determine which warrior would be granted which coup and the honors of the raid. The scalp pole was heavy as the new scalps were added and the dancing went on far into the night until the drummers gave in to their fatigue and the drums stilled.

White Eagle went to his tipi, the largest in the camp, one with a white eagle head painted prominently on the outside.

He met his newest bride, Slender Pecan, but saw that her belly had not yet begin to swell. He hoped she was pregnant with his son. White Eagle had two daughters by his three former wives, but no sons. A chief should have sons.

His third wife had been killed several months ago. Now he had taken a new third wife, who was only fifteen, but who had two brothers and had been raised around men. She would understand the ways of men and conceive for him a son. It must be so. His only other hope was the captive boy, Danny. The small one was only three years, but already he was taking quickly to the Comanche ways. He had his own bow and arrows, and knew many Comanche words even though he had been in camp less than two months. Perhaps Danny would have to be the son of his old age.

White Eagle woke up Laughing Golden Hair. She was a beautiful little girl, even though she was a white captive and had skin the shade of a spring white flower, and hair stolen from the sun.

"We talk English," he said to her. Laughing at him as she awoke, Golden Hair giggled and smiled at him.

"How many horses do you have?" she asked in English. It took her several minutes to get across the meaning of the sentence. The horse word was easy, but "how many" and "you have" were harder. At last he understood the sentence, and he repeated it several times as a question.

But she asked him again. "I want to know how many," she said crossly. He frowned. "How many?" she asked. She held up her hands showing ten fingers, closed them up. "Ten, twenty, thirty?" At last he understood.

He opened and closed his hands ten times.

"A hundred horses!" Laughing Golden Hair said, surprised.

The head of the White Eagle band nodded and said his favorite English word. "Maybe." Then he tucked the five year old white girl into her buffalo robe and went to his own bed made up off the ground.

Slender Pecan lay there waiting for him. She had removed the last of her clothes and was ready. She knew he would be eager to plant more seed when he returned. White Eagle indeed had been eager and four times he tried to plant the seeds of a son in his youngest wife.

Slender Pecan smiled as he went to sleep. This time. This time she was sure that she had conceived a male heir for the leader of the White Eagle band.

White Eagle lay beside the slender woman-child. Lately he had been more and more troubled by the white eyes, and the Pony Soldiers. Why did the whites continually harass them, keep forcing them to move farther and farther west?

This was the People's land. It had been for as long as the oldest grandfather could remember, and as long as their father's fathers could remember.

Why do they try to kill us?

The whites are the invaders of our land, our home, our hunting grounds where we wander and hunt and live as we choose. The whites are the violators of our culture, and our way of life.

Still they come, pushing us farther and farther. One day, White Eagle knew, he must gather all the Comanche nation together and the People would sweep the Comanche hunting grounds clean of the whites. They would burn down every fort, kill every Pony Soldier. They would burn the houses and ranches of the settlers and kill them or drive them eastward even as the Comanches were pushed to the west.

Some day he would do this good thing. But until then the People must remain strong and multiply. The whites bred like rats, with six, eight, even twelve children to a lodge.

He turned over and stroked the sleek body beside him. Yes, he would talk about his grand plan the next time he went to his cousins, the Mesquite Band. It would be a growing plan to return the Comanche to his traditional grounds.

2

Fort Comfort was one of the Indian "pacification installations" which had been built a hundred and twenty miles due west of Austin, in 1865 and two years later, it was not finished. Fort Comfort sat serene and alone on the great Edwards Plateau of Western Texas as a lonely outpost in the continuing battle with the Indians, in this region almost exclusively Comanche.

The fort itself was built in the shape of a large square and had been named as a "wilderness fort" since there had been no settlers or ranchers within a hundred miles of it when construction began. That was no longer the case. Two months earlier, five settler families had moved in less than two miles from the fort and established homesteads.

Three and a half sides of the large fort were completed. The basic construction was adobe blocks, a tough, native Texas clay that could be formed into blocks roughly twelve by eighteen by four. They were formed in wooden molds, let set overnight and then removed to cure in the hot sun. When baked dry they were tougher than red fired brick, or so the Texans said.

The blocks were laid up with adobe mortar into a wall two feet thick at the base and tapering upward, depending on the masons working. The resulting barricade was thick enough to stop any Indian arrow or rifle ball and some said it could bounce off a five-inch army cannon round as well.

The walls inside the fort were a foot thick and paralleled the outside walls, creating a twenty-four foot wide building. This area was cut up into rooms all the way around the inside wall and outfitted as quarters or offices or tack rooms and barracks as needed.

Each side of the fort was three hundred feet long. Roofs consisted of beams of either logs or lumber, then inch-thick sheeting and tarpaper over that. Then a two-foot thick layer of soil went on top of the tarpaper and was covered with native sod to provide a dry, solid and insulated roof from the hot Texas summer sun.

The outer walls over the roofline were three feet higher than the roof to afford troopers a parapet to fire over if they were attacked.

At Fort Comfort, named for Amos J. Comfort, Major General, U.S. Army Retired, one of the corner areas of the fort had not been completed. This section would eventually be used for the tack room, the fort smithy, inside stables and the future sutler's expanded store.

This southeast corner of the fort was still a mass

of adobe bricks, trowels and foundations. The south wall of the fort continued past the unfinished section to the center where the gate was situated that led into the fort's paddock. The paddock extended the full three hundred feet outside the south wall and was built with four strands of smooth wire and sturdy posts which kept the U.S. Army mounts controlled and available at short notice.

The whole west wing of the fort was for officers, their quarters and their mess. Married and single officers lived there with some rooms for transients and guests of the post. There were now only three married officers living on post.

The north side of the quad was for enlisted men's quarters, consisting of a barracks, a day room and a mess in the far corner.

Around on the start of the east wing was situated the kitchen, ordinance shops, guardhouse and the quartermaster's piles of goods and supplies. On the roof over the quartermaster and next to the main gate, stood the guard's lookout tower, built twenty feet above the fort roof.

The main gate was on the east side and beyond that lay the unfinished section, about a hundred feet to the corner. Some days a squad of ten men worked at laying up the adobe blocks, some days they did not. Finishing the fort wall was not high on the Fort Commander's list of jobs to be done.

Captain Colt Harding commanded Fort Comfort. He stood just a little over six feet and weighed one hundred eighty five pounds. He was lean and fit, with short cropped brown hair, brown eyes under heavy brows and lately he had gone to a thick, full moustache. He liked it.

The captain walked out of his quarters and office on the west side of the quad that morning about ten o'clock and watched the visitors arrive. Today the courier was due from Austin, but this was not only a courier but a huge supply train of twenty wagons, and an escort of thirty troopers. There seemed to be a half dozen officers with the group, which also was unusual.

A young first lieutenant rode up to the small porch where Captain Harding stood. He snapped a salute and received one in return.

"Lieutenant Jefferson, reporting to the commanding officer with a supply train, thirty replacement troopers, and six officers for your command."

"Lieutenant Jefferson! I'm struck dumb. We've been waiting for new officers for six months. Welcome aboard. Bring the new gentlemen to my quarters for a proper welcome."

Lieutenant Riddle came to the door, looked out and smiled. He waved at the new officer and walked toward the wagon train. "I better get things put away here, Captain." He took over and quickly had B Company unloading the wagons at the quartermaster's doors, then placing the rest of the goods in vacant quarters.

The six officers trooped into the captain's office where he had a bottle of six year old Kentucky sipping whiskey he had been saving for an occasion.

They had slapped dust off their new uniforms outside, doffed their hats and lined up in the office.

Captain Harding went down the line, staring at each man intently as he shook his hand. Each name and some distinguishing characteristic was burned at once into Harding's mind. He'd never forget the name or the tag.

"First Lieutenant Lucas Jefferson, sir. Sorry no relation to the President."

Harding took his hand. A firm, steady grip, square cut face with a soft grin, at ease, about five-ten and sure of himself. A strong leader. Harding moved to the next man.

"First Lieutenant Marvin George, Sir. Delighted to be here."

The captain shook his hand, a little weak but not limp. He wore a pencil thin moustache, longer side-burns. A precise man who might be well placed in the quartermaster slot that had been vacant for six months.

At each the captain said something innocuous and moved on.

"Lieutenant Wendel Musgrove, sir. I'm looking forward to some real action."

Captain looked at him again. He was nearly six feet, with a full beard carefully trimmed, a steel blue glint in his eyes and a hard handshake. This might be the commander of the Lightning Company.

The next man was about five-seven, a little over-weight, looked soft. He had a gentle handshake and looked his commander in the eyes almost apologeti-cally.

"Lieutenant Herman Schultz, sir. Formerly with the infantry, looking forward to this assignment."

I bet you are, Harding thought as he moved on.

"Lt. Ezekiel Odemark, sir. My first regular posting. I'll do my best, sir."

"That's all any of us can do."

The last man was tall and split rail thin. He had red hair and freckles, wore eyeglasses. He looked relaxed and sure of himself, as if he'd seen all of this before and tolerated it. An interesting reaction.

"Sir. Lieutenant Vance Petroff. Yes, I'm a bit old to be a shavetail, but, sir, I came up through the ranks and have my West Point ring. I'm glad to be here."

Captain Harding shook his hand as well, liking the tall up from the ranks officer immediately. Lieutenent Riddle arrived with the glasses and poured the whiskey. They all lifted their first drink together and the captain gave the toast.

"To God and Country, to the Second Cavalry, to Fort Comfort." They all drank. Ten minutes later the new officers were sent to find their quarters Lieutenant Riddle had arranged. He told them there might be some changes made in the next few days, but they should settle in. The captain would see them for the evening meal.

At noon Lieutenant Riddle reported to Harding that the three day patrol sweeping the western sector had not arrived back at the appointed time. Eleven o'clock had been the expected return hour.

By two o'clock Harding showed his worry. Edwards led the patrol. But sometimes even the best officer can get into trouble.

"Lieutenant Riddle, send out three four man patrols to sweep a six mile area out as far as they can reach by dark, then return. If any hostiles are seen they are to return at once and report. There is to be no engagement unless it is forced. Don't use any of the Lightning Company. Get them moving."

Captain Harding sat at his desk. He had been trying to figure where to use his wealth of new officers. He had not had a command so nearly full of officers in years. He had ignored the dispatch case Lieutenent Jefferson had brought him. Now he unstrapped it and dumped out the large envelopes. There were four of them. One caught his eye. It said in red lettering: "Promotions!"

He slit it open and the top sheet of paper had his immediate attention.

"Promotions approved and authorized by the Congress of the United States and the Generals of the army include the following men under my command." It was signed Colonel Philip Sparkman, Commanding.

"Captain Colt B. Harding, 14875, promoted to major.

"Lieutenant John B. Riddle, 16394, promoted to captain."

Colt Harding sat back in his chair and stared at the piece of paper. Just after the war, he had not been certain whether to stay in the army. He had been cut down to a captain, and it had taken him two years to battle through to a major—even so that was about four years quicker than the normal time. He was pleased.

He was just as pleased to see John get his captain epaulets. He would find a spare pair from his own blouse and present them to John. Colt hurried into the outer office, but the adjutant wasn't there.

"Corporal Swenson, would you find Lieutenent Riddle for me. There's something I need to tell him right away." Swenson, the orderly and clerk for Major Harding, hurried out the door. He knew Riddle was back with the quartermaster supplies, getting everything put away promptly and locked up.

Harding went to his desk and looked at the other papers in the promotion folder. He was authorized to promote six men to sergeant, and three to corporal, if such Table of Organization posts were open. Also any sergeants or corporals killed in action during the past six months, could be replaced in addition to the above quota.

When Harding checked his watch it was slightly after three o'clock. He went out to the lookout tower, climbed the ladder outside the guardhouse to the roof. The troopers came to attention as he entered.

"At ease. Have you seen anything of the six man patrol due back at eleven?"

"No sir, Captain. The search teams went out most an hour ago. Everyone's out of sight by now."

Major Harding bobbed his head. "Send word to me the moment you see anyone riding this direction."

"Yes sir."

Major Harding returned to his quarters. Lieutenant Riddle was at his desk sorting out the manifests on the shipment. It was the biggest one he could remember.

"We've got supplies now we should have had last spring," he said, frustration oozing from his pores.

"You think you have problems, Lieutenant, come look at my desk. Papers scattered all over it."

They went into the office, and Major Harding took a pair of gold captain's insignia shoulder patches from his desk drawer and handed them to Riddle.

"Congratulations, Captain Riddle!"

He showed him the paper.

"My god, it finally happened! I hope you didn't write this out as a joke."

"I can't sign the old man's name that way," Harding said.

" . . . and you're a major! Well done!" They gripped hands firmly.

"Been a long time coming, John. You deserved it. Know what else I'm doing? One of those six new officers is going to be our Quartermaster Officer. Get that mess off your back so you can sharpen up this post and get some training done."

"Marksmanship? Even Colonel Sparkman has said it's a waste of good ammunition."

"He won't after I show him the Lightning Company in action. We need more training, more live firing practice."

He stood and paced to the door, then back. "What the hell could have happened to Lieutenant Edwards and that routine patrol? He's the best field officer we have."

By nightfall none of the search teams had come back. Major Harding announced his promotion to the officer's mess, and he was toasted. Then back in his office, the major and his new adjutant captain looked over the sector Edwards was to patrol. It was due west, stretching about thirty miles to the southwest, then a thirty mile march due north, and the return thirty mile ride back to the fort on a southeast azimuth.

"Those search teams could get out about twenty miles before dark," Major Harding said. "I'm betting they found nothing. Alert the Lightning Company. We'll be riding at five A.M. We'll split the company into two units. I'll lead one to the return route of the patrol. I want Captain Kenny from A Company to lead the other unit on the outbound route. Send Sergeant Casemore with him. Get things moving."

Major Harding spent another hour with Captain

Edwards trying to slot the new officers into the fort's roster. They decided they needed to know a little more about each man first. They had the officer's file on each from Colonel Sparkman, but it didn't tell them enough.

"Jefferson and George should be considered for leading the Lightning Company," Captain Riddle said. "You shouldn't be doing all the work there. I'll take anybody on as Quartermaster Officer, except Lieutenant Schultz."

"I thought you were taken with the young man at once," Harding said grinning. "Not sure what the hell we'll do with him. Put him in as platoon leader with Captain Kenny. Maybe he can turn the young man into an officer."

Major Harding leaned back in his chair and rubbed his eyes. "You know what I'm thinking from that first talk and from dinner tonight? I might go with Petroff. He has the style, the guts, the kind of drive that the Lightning team needs."

"He's a junior second lieutenant."

"Don't give a damn. If he's the best man for the job, he gets it, regulations be damned."

They both laughed. Each had said the same line a dozen times about one thing or the other lately.

"You get through the rest of the dispatches?"

"Not by an envelope full. You can look at them tomorrow. I have an early reveille. Oh, write up an order promoting Lance Swenson to sergeant as of this date. He's overdue as well."

"Damned sure."

Major Harding looked at his promotion orders, smiled and then went into his lonely quarters. His wife was still everywhere. A cup, a picture, a vase. A hundred things reminded him of her. She had been cut down by Comanches less than four months ago when she and their two children were on their way from Austin to Fort Comfort.

His wife, Milly, and son, Yale, had been killed along with thirteen troopers. His baby girl, Sadie, kidnapped by White Eagle and his band. The time of reckoning was coming closer. He would work out a way—somehow—to get Sadie back. First he had to get his command settled down—and find out what happened to Edwards and his six man scouting patrol.

He fell into bed and blew out the lamp and went to sleep almost at once.

By daylight the next morning, Major Harding and the first two squads of Lightning Company were nearly ten miles from camp. They moved at a canter working northwest on the return leg the patrol should have taken.

The search teams had returned just before midnight. Sergeant Swenson had wakened Harding and told him. They established they had moved out about eighteen miles but none of the teams found any sign of the scouting patrol. It was as Major Harding had feared.

Now they moved along at their usual lightning pace. Each man on short rations for the day. They had two Indian scouts along from habit. There would be no need for hunting on this trip to provide food for the Lightning units.

Slightly after ten A.M., they passed the thirty mile mark on the northwest sighting and swung due south. They had ridden a little more than ten miles when they saw buzzards circling. Major Harding saw them first and slowed the pace. If the buzzards were there, then there was no chance anyone was left alive. There was little point in rushing now.

A half hour later they came on the scene. Two dead horses lay on the barren land near the water course and the two-foot cut where one trooper lay dead. They found the others scattered toward the rock outcroppings a hundred yards away.

All of the bodies were naked, slashed and maimed, some with hacked off hands and feet, and with stabs and gashes made by lances. The Comanche believed that the slain men's spirits would carry the identical crippling into the afterlife and not be such skilled opponents if they had to fight them again.

Their clothes, boots and weapons were gone. The two dead horses were both Indian ponies. The army mounts had been taken away.

Major Harding fired three shots in the air to try to attract the attention of the other half of the company under Captain Kenny. Then he sent his two Tonkawa scouts in a half mile circle around the position to try to locate any trail that the Comanche had left.

Hatchet, the chief scout, returned before the troopers had been gathered and readied for bural in side by side graves. Major Harding rode with him over a small rise to a spot trampled down and littered with horse droppings. It didn't take a scout to tell a big herd had been held here.

"Horses, maybe hundred, two hundred. Wait here two, three hours."

"Stolen horses from a Comanche raid?"

Hatchet nodded.

"Where? We haven't had word of any raid nearby."

Hatchet looked south, then north, then south

again.

"Mexico," he said. "Over border. Comanche long time ago raid over border. Much easy."

"Hatchet, I want you to backtrack the Comanche. Find out for sure if they came from Mexico. When you're certain, come back here and track them to their camp. They might be on one last buffalo hunt before they go to winter camp. Find them. Then come back and report to me."

The Tonkawa Indian nodded, motioned to the other Tonkawa and they rode off south.

Back at the graves, Major Harding read a simple ceremony from a folded page from the field manaul he took from his pocket. He walked around the area, looking for broken arrows, spent casings. Quickly he reconstructed the battle. The patrol had been surprised, driven to the cliff and the shallow protection. The Indians might have "rained" arrows on them until they decided to make a try for the rocks. They never made it. At least they had gone down fighting. That sounded like Lieutenant Edwards.

As the last of the troopers was buried, Captain Kenny rode up with his troops.

They took what few personal effects they had found, and began the long ride back to Fort Comfort. Captain Riddle was going to have to write the seven letters to the troopers' last of kin. Colt Harding had written too many of them lately. He was angry at losing so many good men.

As they rode toward the fort, cutting across country in a miles saving route, Major Harding was trying out officers in the slots on his troops personnel board. Somehow, names and positions kept getting mixed up.

Then he began thinking about Sadie. Finding out

where she was had to be his first and overriding priority. He only had two months before the snow flew. Long before that, White Eagle would take his band into a winter camp where as many as five to seven hundred other warriors would camp with their families and their herds of horses. If they got to a winter camp, he wouldn't have a chance to rescue Sadie until Spring.

It had to be soon, damn soon.

3

When the Lightning Company returned to Fort Comfort just before dark, the men had covered sixty-five miles, buried seven troopers, and had lost a lot of friends. There was a quietness when they came into the front gate. Everyone knew what must have happened when they saw no wounded, no bodies, no extra horses.

Comanches!

The word spread around the fort quickly. The Lightning Company was given late chow, and Major Harding huddled with Captain Riddle.

He explained how the battle had probably gone.

"Far as I can tell, the Comanche must have figured that the patrol would see the raiding party and the stolen horses, so they attacked first. Damn smart of them, and it worked."

Captain Riddle looked at the roster of dead men.

He had crossed out Edwards name on the organization chart he held.

"Death can come so damn sudden out here," he said softly. "It can sneak up on you when you think everything is settled down and peaceful."

Major Harding went to the small stove and poured a fresh cup of coffee for himself, then brought the pot to the captain's outstretched cup.

"Could you write the letters this time, John? I'd appreciate it."

Captain Riddle nodded. He shuffled the papers again and put out a new organization chart showing the new officers in various slots.

"Take a look at this. Just a suggestion."

Harding looked over the assignments for the new officers. He nodded, "Yes, I want Petroff with the Lightning Company. Schultz with Captain Kenny where he can't hurt anything." He stared at the other names.

"Let's put Lieutenant Jefferson in Lieutenant Edward's old spot with Lieutenant Musgrove as his second, and Lieutenant George can serve under Lieutenant Young with C Company. Write up the assignment, then we're going to get in some hard work before the scouts get back. We have to make some response to this. Whichever band it was is going to feel some U.S. Cavalry steel and ball."

They worked for another hour getting the paperwork ready, assigning the enlisted men to various companies to equalize them in strength. There would be another competition for men to join the Lightning Company if and when there were vacancies. So far they had suffered no casualties nor had anyone asked to go back to a regular company. Harding wanted ten more men who could qualify and be trained quickly to fill in when needed.

He went to see Mrs. Edwards. She was in bed, her face swollen from crying. Mrs. Kenny was with her. He talked with Mrs. Edwards for a few minutes and she said she wanted to get back to Austin and then to Ohio just as quickly as she could. She had suffered enough from the Army to last her a lifetime. At least Ben, her older son would not remember any of this.

"Yes, Ma'am. I understand your loss. I'll arrange an escort to leave at ten in the morning if that's satisfactory. You'll have a twenty man escort to Austin. We'll arrange a cover on one of the freight wagons. It's a hard five day trip by wagon, Mrs. Edwards."

"I know, I came out here that way," she snapped. Then she began crying again. "I'm sorry, Major. I'm ashamed, and sorry and . . . and . . . Oh damnit! Why did he have to die?"

Mrs. Kenny motioned and Major Harding went out of the bedroom. Mrs. Kenny followed.

"She'll be ready to go by tomorrow," Mrs. Kenny said softly. "Poor dear has really taken this hard. We all think our husbands are indestructible, that they'll last forever. It's hard to accept this." She glanced up. "But then you know what I'm talking about much better than I do. I'll be sure that she's ready to go."

Back in his office, Major Harding called the new officers and told them about their assignments. He went over their service records and explained why they were being put in specific jobs. Most of them agreed with the reasoning.

Harding saved Lieutenant Petroff for the last. The officer stood at ease in front of his commanding officer.

"Petroff, I want you to move in as second in command of the Lightning Company. As soon as I think you're ready, you'll take over the group. Have you heard about our Lightning brigade?"

"Yes, sir. Everybody at San Antonio has heard about it. Sir, it seems like you've caused quite a fuss with the new Indian fighting tactics."

"Nothing new about them at all, Lieutenant. The Indians have been fighting us that way for years. That's why they are winning, and we're stalemated."

"Yes, sir."

Major Harding smiled. "Petroff, did you by any chance take a field commission during the war?"

"Yes, sir, but I got them to leave that out of my records. It wasn't much. I was a captain for about a year, then got cut down to sergeant."

"Why West Point?"

"Figured I was stuck in the army, and the officers get paid the most, get the best food, best quarters, and have the most fun. Why not be an officer?"

"Good reasoning. But remember, in my outfit, the officers also work the hardest, have the toughest decisions to make, shoulder the most responsibility, and have to write letters to the next of kin whenever a man is killed in action in their company."

"Yes, sir. I've done some of all of that."

"Good. Petroff, what I'm trying to develop here is the best damn fighting machine the U.S. Army has ever seen. The men and I are shaping this outfit to the exact job we need to do. We don't take equipment we don't need just because the regulations say we should. We don't go by the book. We meet the needs of the job at hand. If that means traveling light so we can cover eighty-five miles in twenty-four hours with two hours for rest, we do it."

"I agree with the idea, Major."

"Good. This company also trains two days a week. Tomorrow is training day. Right now I want you to go over to the Lightning Company barracks and get acquainted with your men. Tell them you came up from enlisted, went to the Point, and that you'll know the first and last name of all forty men in the company within forty-eight hours."

"Reckon I can do that, Major."

"Good, get out of here and get to work."

"Yes, sir." He turned and started to leave.

"Soldier, don't you salute your commanding officer when you're dismissed?"

Petroff turned, and a slow smile spread over his face.

"Yes, sir, if it helps meet the need of the job at hand."

Colt Harding laughed. He hadn't laughed so hard in weeks. He grinned at the new man and waved at him. "Get out of here, Petroff, I think you and I are going to get along just fine."

When Petroff left, Major Harding spent ten minutes looking at the big map of Western Texas that took up half of one wall. He put a pin in the place where the patrol had been wiped out and looked south. The hostiles very well could have been coming up from Mexico. If so, where were they headed?

There were several pins in the maps just north of the ambush point where Comanches had camped before, summer spots, hunting camps. But all were closer than he figured the band would be stopping. If it had been White Eagle, Harding imagined the

Comanche would be camped far to the north, well up on the Wichita or even the Peace River. He wasn't sure. That would have to wait until Hatchet came back from his scouting trip.

How long? Two or three more days? Maybe five or six. He had to wait. Only then could he figure out if he could follow the murdering Comanches and attack. Hatchet was well aware of the major's special interest in White Eagle. If he saw the big eagle head on the side of a large tipi, he would be sure and report it.

Major Harding had given Captain Riddle the job of getting Lieutenant Odemark familiar with the duties of the quartermaster, and where the supplies were and how to operate. The quartermaster sergeant would be able to help out the new officer a lot.

The work of selecting enlisted men to promote to corporal and sergeant would be tougher. Captain Riddle would draw up a tentative list for the major's inspection. Usually the company commanders would send up a list, but most of them had so little experience with the men it wouldn't work this time. He was sure Captain Riddle would consult with Captain Kenny of "A" Company and Young in C Company to find the right men.

Colt Harding looked at the map of Western Texas again. Only a few more installations showed west of Fort Worth and Austin. Western Texas was mostly a wide, unsettled expanse of flat plains, a few rolling hills and the high caprock mesa to the far west. Thousands and thousands of square miles where White Eagle could be hiding Sadie.

Damnit! He sat at his desk and tried to write down different ways he could find the only survivor of his family. He had few options. Gossip and stories told by traders who prowled the Indian villages and camps. The few prospectors the Indians permitted to wander the mostly unproductive West Texas. Information from renegades who would sell anything they knew, regardless if it were the truth or not. The missions of his army scouts who were tracking hostiles.

At last he wrote down the last and best chance of finding Sadie: Taking Hatchet and five of his best trackers and warriors, and prowling all the haunts of the Comanche as silently and invisibly as a moonbeam, until he found the White Eagle camp. Then he would have to slip into the camp like a thief, snatch Sadie out of the tipi of the mightiest Comanche warrior and then outrun, out maneuver and out think the savages in their own land and with the manpower odds of twenty to one.

The prospects were so damn gloomy that Colt headed for the medical office, and banged through the door. Corporal Adolph Marlin, jumped up from a small desk and braced at attention.

"At ease, Marlin. Captain Jenkins in?"

"Yes, sir." He stepped to the closest door, knocked and opened the panel. "Captain. Major Harding to see you, sir."

Captain Jenkins was deeply involved in a leather bound book. He looked up, dropped his feet off the table and stood.

"You ailing, Major?"

"Somewhat." He watched the corporal close the door and then grinned at the medic. "You have any of that medicinal brandy?"

"Nope, fresh out, but I have some genuine two year old Tennessee whiskey guaranteed to burn out your tonsils."

"Good. I can use about half of it. You had a busy week?"

"Not so you could notice. Took out an appendix the other day. A little flu, and some blisters and boils."

"Good. You know the medical kit we take with us on the Lightning trips?"

"Yep. I put it together."

"I need one more. Smaller, no larger than a mess kit, light and portable with any basics a body might need on a three, four week ride."

"For how many men?"

"Just one."

Doc Jenkins stared at him hard for a minute. "You fixing to go on another one of them wild rides with a few savages?"

"Might. Unless you can tell me another way to find my Sadie."

Captain Jenkins eyed him coolly for a minute, then shook his head. "I'll get some things together. Do some thinking on it. If you can see you way clear to have supper with me and then invest a few hours in a chess match."

"A few hours? How many games you plan to play?"

"Depends how many times you want to get beaten."

They both grinned and Major Harding left with a nod, saying that he would be back about six.

Across the quad in the small office where Captain Kenny had his A Company orderly room, Second Lieutenant Henry Schultz stared blankly at a sheet of paper with all the names of the troopers in the unit. Captain Kenny had instructed him to memorize the names and attach them to individual soldiers as quickly as possible.

He twisted on the chair in the cramped office. Nobody told him it would be like this. He had bowed to his father's wishes and had struggled through West Point. The first year after graduation there had been no billet open for him. The Army was still overflowing with officers who wished to remain in the service even though they were cut in rank drastically. He knew a full colonel who took a cut to second lieutenant to stay in.

At the end of the second year out of the Point an opening had developed and his colonel father rushed him into it. It had been in ordinance in Washington D.C. and it actually wasn't so bad. More like a regular job. He worked in an office and went home at night. But that office had been closed with the reduction of personnel even two years after the war, and he was sent to Omaha, and then six months later to San Antonio.

He was listed as a field officer, but in truth he had never fired a shot in anger and had no desire to.

Schultz dried off his palms where they had been sweating. His father would have a stroke if Henry applied for resignation from the service. He had his "commitment" after West Point to serve out first, of course. He looked up quickly as Corporal Victor Gregory came up to his desk.

"Lieutenant Schultz, Captain Kenny would like to see you, sir."

Schultz wiped his palms off on the sides of his pants, nodded at the corporal and went into the next small office. He had been told not to salute on such occasions, but he stood stiffly in front of the desk.

"Schultz, for God's sake, relax. When no enlisted

men are around, you and I are informal. Sit down and take it easy."

"Yes, thank you, sir."

"I understand that you've had very little practical field experience."

"None. None whatsoever."

"We'll change that. Tomorrow I'll be leading a sector patrol sweep with ten men. I want you to come along for the experience. In two or three weeks you'll be leading these patrols yourself. Nothing to them really. You made it through West Point, this will be simple. Just keep your eyes open and your defenses ready."

He paused. "What happened to Lieutenant Edwards was the exception. Don't worry about it. Out here we do our best. If we get hit by a war party, we simply outfight them and get back to the fort."

"Usually."

"That's the one part of being a soldier an officer can never worry about. So forget it. There are over seventeen thousand of us out here in the Army of the Missouri."

"Yes, sir. When do we leave tomorrow?"

"Usual time. Oh, you might not know the routine for a patrol day. We'll be gone for most of three days. Our routine goes like this: 4:45 A.M. is first call when the men roll out of their blankets. At 4:55 is reveille and stable call when the men saddle horses and harness any mules being used. At 5:00 is mess call. Each man has a half hour to prepare and eat his meal, the most relaxed time in the morning.

"Then at 5:30 is general call when we strike camp. The troops strike tents and store equipment. In our case we won't take tents on a three day ride.

"At 5:45 boots and saddles is blown and everyone

mounts up. At 5:55 it's fall in as our column assembles in a line of march, usually four horses wide on a full company ride.

"Promptly at six A.M. it's forward march and we begin our movement through our patrol day. Any questions?"

"Will we have an orderly to cook our food?"

Captain Kenny laughed. "That we will, Schultz, we'll use mine and simply double the portions. He's a fine lad and a good cook. Actually he's our clerk, Corporal Greggory."

"Thank you, Captain. I should get back to my quarters and start getting my gear ready. If there's nothing else I need to do."

"No, go ahead. See you at mess."

Second Lieutenant Herman Schultz went directly to his quarters. His was a bachelor arrangement and he was the only person in the two small rooms. He locked the door, hurried into the bedroom and threw himself on the bed. Almost at once he began to shiver and then shake.

It was a half hour before he could control himself enough to sit up on the edge of the bed. He was afraid he was going to urinate in his pants. With a great deal of effort he went to the officer's latrine near the paddock, and made it back to his door.

Inside, he nearly collapsed against the closed door. Sweat boiled from his face. There was not a chance he could go to the officer's mess looking like this. He had to battle out the fear now, and be calm and ready for the patrol in the morning.

As he thought of it, and the seven graves out there on the prairie where the men from the last three day patrol lay, he shivered more and more. He nearly fell getting to his bed. Then he dropped on the blanket, fully clothed and knew that it would take a firing squad to force him off that bed.

He was missing the officers' mess. That was good, the very idea of food made him sick to his stomach.

Schultz rolled on his side, drew his knees up almost to his chest in a fetal ball and quietly began to sob.

In Captain Jenkins's quarters, the dinner dishes had been removed and the first chess game was over. The medical staff had won.

Now Major Harding pounded his tin cup on the heavy wooden table and held it up. They had given up on glasses after three had been broken amid great laughter and blame aimed at the other one.

"Damnit, Jim, where the hell's the rest of the whiskey?"

"Damn bottle developed a hole in it," Doctor Jenkins wheezed. "All the fucking whiskey ran out the hole." He paused. "The hole was on top of the bottle!" Dr. Jenkins broke up laughing, nearly fell down, but found a second bottle in the small cupboard of his quarters and unstoppered it. He poured in a finger of whiskey.

"Just getting started, Doc. Keep pouring." Colt Harding bellowed. He was drunk. He knew he was drunk and he was glad. He didn't tie on a drinking bout often, but when he did he always made sure he had medical attention nearby.

Some men get mean when they drink, some curl up in a corner and wail and cry, some stare into the distance, others even become monotonously eloquent. When he drank too much, Major Colt Harding revealed his fondest dreams and hopes.

The third game of chess was destined never to be finished. Colt kept telling Doc Jenkins how he was going to rescue his baby, his little girl, Sadie. Doc kept telling Harding how he had been squeezed out of a hospital just forming in Boston and that he damn well should have been the director now.

"Never did tell you about Boston Medical, did I, Colt?" He stared at his commander.

"About a thousand damn times you told me," Colt whispered, but Doc Jenkins didn't hear him.

"This damn young kid from New York came up and married Betty Lou, and her father *damn well bought the kid* the number one spot on the hospital staff. Made him staff director, and he'd only been a surgeon for three years.

"Made everybody mad. I had a small fisticuffs fight with him one night and the next day I was out on my medical ass. Couldn't get a job in Boston, so I chucked the whole damn town and joined the army as a surgeon. Fixed the little whip shit!"

"You sure did, Doc. Fixed him good. Just the way I'm gonna fix that damn savage, White Eagle. He's a hostile. Hell, I'll slip up on him with about twenty of my Lighting men and we'll stomp him into the ground. We'll pick up Sadie and carry her out and let her pick the best pony in the whole fucking Comanche herd, and we'll ride out and thumb our asses at old White Eagle!"

Doc took his turn and became sadder with each telling, and Major Harding became more positive and sure of his plan to rescue Sadie every time he repeated the scheme.

It was nearly two A.M. when the second bottle of booze somehow became empty and the two soldiers walked to the door holding each other up.

An hour later one of the interior guards saw Major Harding leaning against the wall outside Doc's office. He carried his commanding officer to his quarters. The door was not locked.

Once inside, Major Harding got control of himself a little more, thanked the guard and fell on his bed.

It was past reveille when he woke up, still in his uniform, chilled and stiff and with a pounding headache. He poured water in a basin and splashed it on his face until his head started to clear.

"Never touch that damned rotgut again as long as I live," he mumbled. What day was it? Tuesday, Wednesday? Another day to wait for the scouts to come back. He stared in the mirror. His hand shook as he tried to shave in cold water.

A moment later he heard someone moving around in his office. Sergeant Swenson would be there getting a fire going. Good. He'd heat water and shave hot. What day was this? He'd been through that. Yeah, it would be a day of training for the Lightning Company. A chance to show Lieutenant Petroff what his men could do, and what he'd have to be able to do as well.

He had a vague memory of some grand plans about how he would rescue Sadie. He had told Doc Jenkins last night. Hard as he might try, he couldn't remember the plan.

4

Sadie Harding, called Laughing Golden Hair by her Comanche captives, had just turned five years old. She sat near the entrance to the big tipi with the white eagle painted on it and hit the rock again and again at the flat rock in front of her.

Sadie and every other able bodied woman and girl in White Eagle's band were busy making pemmican. If they made enough, they would have plenty to eat all winter through. If they did not make enough, there would be hunger and starvation. That was motivation for everyone in the tribe.

Weeks ago the warriors and hunters had brought down the giant, shaggy beasts, then all those in the tribe cut up the meat into long thin strips and hung them on drying racks so the sun would preserve them.

The jerky was saved and when they had time, they

began making pemmican from the jerky. First it was pounded into a powder and then mixed with buffalo fat. That was the staple food, but the Comanches usually mixed in other foods to flavor it.

Persimmons were the favorite. First these had to be beaten into a pulp with sticks so the seeds could be separated from the pulp. The pulp was then formed into cakes, usually on a flat rock, and the cakes left to dry in the sun. The cakes would be kept until time to use them in the pemmican.

Many other fruits and nuts were used as well to mix into pemmican to make it taste better. Sadie had used grapes and plums that had been dried and stored in bags. She knew that wild cherries, walnuts and pecans were also favorites of the Comanche to mix into their pemmican, whenever they could find them.

The pemmican would be stored in rawhide boxes and cases called parfleches. In these strong and waterproof boxes, the pemmican lasted for months. It was nutritious and the one staple an Indian tribe counted on for wintering over. It was the only way the hunting tribes had to preserve food.

Sadie worked beside Doris, the last white woman the Comanche had captured. White Eagle claimed her, hoping that she might produce for him a son. The white women were known to bear children often and easily.

Doris had been a wife and mother in a five family settlement. The men had pushed westward into "better land" and beyond any real protection of the Army or civilians. The Comanche knew they were there, and one day swept down on them and killed everyone except Doris and a young boy, Danny. Then burned down the houses and barns and drove off all the livestock.

Raiding and stealing women, children and horses was not considered by the Comanche warriors to be either right or wrong. This was simply what they did for a living, it was what they trained for from their youth and what they lived for. Raiding or conducting war against the whites or their Indian enemies was their normal activity.

Doris was only 19 when she was captured. She knew she was fortunate. She was a slave, but White Eagle, the leader of the whole band, treated her much as he did his three wives. She slept inside the tipi, she had clothes and robes and ate with everyone else.

Curiously, she had not been repelled or disgusted by White Eagle's first sexual advances. Making love with her husband had always excited Doris, and she quickly found out that this strange "savage" was even more thrilling for her when he came to her bed.

Even so, she knew she had to escape and take Sadie and little Danny with her. Somehow, sometime. Her long black hair had been carefully braided down each side so she looked Indian. Her skin had tanned to a creamy brown, covering the few freckles.

"Sadie, you're the best pemmican maker we have," Doris said to the young girl softly in English. They talked English more now, since White Eagle was learning to speak the language.

"I'm getting tired," Sadie said. She looked up with her soft, blue eyes. "Is it true if we don't make enough pemmican now, that we'll starve to death this winter?"

"I'm afraid it is true, Sadie. When the snow is

deep, there will be no wild animals to hunt and little fresh meat. We'll have to live off the pemmican. I like it flavored with the persimmons best I think."

"I like them all." Sadie stood. "I think I'll go throw stones in the water. I won't be able to do that either when the stream freezes over this winter."

She stood and ran off toward the river. No one told her to come back. No one scolded her or spanked her. Doris had been amazed at how the Comanches raised their children. She had never seen a child disciplined, never spanked, never slapped. There was virtually no criticism at all of the children.

Most had small chores to do around the campsite, but when these were done they could do almost anything they wanted to. The most critical word spoken to a Comanche child was to stop him or her from doing something and tell the child, "That is not the way the People do things."

With this in mind, Doris was certain that she had never seen happier, better disciplined and more loving children. She didn't know how to explain it. She heard Danny crying and looked up quickly. The other women in the tipi had left Danny's care up to her. He was difficult for them, since he missed his parents and what was familiar. He was only three and it was taking him longer to adapt to the Comanche way of life than some of the other stolen children. The five new Mexican children were fitting into the life of the camp quickly.

She went to him, slipping inside the big tipi. It was the largest in the camp, more than 16 feet across. The fire ring was in the center so the smoke could rise through the smoke flap fifteen feet above. Around the edges of the tipi the tough buffalo hide had been left long enough so it lapped over inside.

The beds were put on this so no wind could blow under the edge.

There was much more room in the tipi than she had in her cabin. It took a little getting used to, but now she saw that generations of use had taught the Comanches how to utilize the tipi to the best possible extent.

She found Danny waking up from a nap. She hurried him out to the relief point in the woods behind the tipi, and then sang to him, put on his tiny breechclout, and took him back to the front of the tipi where he could play in the grass where a few dry leaves were dropping.

Doris knew that if she were going to find a way to escape it had to be before they went to their winter camp. Two weeks, maybe three more, were all she had. Most of that time would be taken up with the last big hunt of the season. How could she do it?

Sadie had a bow and arrow that one of the older boys had given her. He had outgrown it and had a new one. She fitted the tough buffalo sinew string into the notches at the end of the bow and tested it.

The bow was too hard for her to pull all the way, but she grinned when she could pull it a little farther this time. She notched an arrow, and stood the way she had seen the boys do, and pulled back the string.

She let go before she wanted to because she could not hold it any longer. The arrow shot forward and stuck in the tree she had aimed at. Sadie was so happy she whooped for joy, and three young girls hurried over to see what she was excited about. Then for an hour the three had a contest to see who could hit the tree. They all were about six, and none of them hit the tree again.

At last they gave up and launched leaves in the small stream in front of the camp, and then threw stones at the "canoes" until they sank them.

The girls then linked arms and ran through the camp, tipping over a small rack of drying buffalo meat. They hooted and laughed as the three women nearby calmly left their work and straightened the rack, hanging the meat back in place and kicking away the dogs and puppies that swarmed around.

They did not shout at the children. They simply repaired the damage and went back to making pemmican. There was no need to be angry. The women remembered when they too had been six years old and went running through the camps.

Black Bird, one of White Eagle's daughters, and best friend of Sadie, tugged at the younger girl and they ran to a tipi set a little to one side, deeper into the fringe of woods behind the stream.

Sitting on a log in front of his tipi was Runs Plenty. He was so old nobody could remember his age. He sat on the log, his watery eyes peering down the length of an arrow.

Laughing Golden Hair knew Runs Plenty was famous in the band as the best arrowmaker in Texas. Laughing Golden Hair looked at the bundles of dogwood shoots that hung on the outside of the tipi and from various trees nearby. They were seasoning until they were just right. Many more bundles were hung from pegs and rawhide strips inside the tipi where the smoke and heat from the fire helped to season the wood until it was ready to be made into arrows.

The girls watched, silently, with a great deal of respect as the old man twirled a bow-like lathe that was the first step in trueing the shafts. He worked slowly, patiently, his hands feeling for uneven places his eyes could no longer find. Again and again a small boy pulled the rawhide strip that twirled the bow so Runs Plenty could work on the dogwood shaft.

When he had it worked the best he could, Runs Plenty felt the shaft. When he found a rough or crooked place, he rubbed it with buffalo fat. Next he drew the shaft slowly through two grooved sandstone slabs. They had been carefully chiseled out until they formed a perfectly straight mold when put together. The shaft was pulled through the mold several times until Runs Plenty was satisfied.

Then he tapered it exactly so with a treasured piece of pumice stone that sanded it down the way he wanted.

Sadie watched with fascination as the old Indian worked on his arrows. Once he reached out and touched her braided blonde hair and said something quickly to Black Bird. She giggled and told Laughing Golden Hair that Runs Plenty said her hair had been stolen from a new born sun.

Runs Plenty took the tapered arrow and pulled it through a round hole he had cut in a tough disc of bone. He had left a sharp spur projecting from one side of the hole. This sliced out a groove as the arrow was pulled forward.

Four grooves were made in each arrow. Two were perfectly straight along the shaft. These allowed blood to run out of the wound to kill the animal quicker.

The second two grooves were curved slightly when Runs Plenty turned his wrist as he pulled the arrow through. The straight grooves were painted black and the curved ones red.

Black Bird explained that the grooves kept the

arrow from warping in months to come.

Black Bird wanted to go, but Sadie held her arm. She had never seen Runs Plenty work on arrows before.

The old man rubbed the shaft now until it gleamed with hand polish, but that was not the last step. Next an arrowhead had to be made. The Comanches did not use flint arrowheads anymore. They made them by laboriously cutting them from barrel hoops or other metal stolen from the white men. Then they used the files they had bartered for from the traders to sharpen the points and finish forming them. When they were ready, they were heated, then dropped into cold water to make them so hard they would bounce off a rock.

Sometimes the traders brought ready-made arrowheads. A dozen of them could be traded for only one buffalo robe. The Indians didn't know the trader paid only half a cent each for the arrowheads, and he would sell the buffalo robe for ten dollars at his next stop.

Each warrior had his own mark on an arrow. Sometimes the arrowmaker painted it on, sometimes the warrior did. It might be one red circle, or a black one. Three black dashes, or two, or a triangle or diamond. In a large band there might be a hundred different markings for a hundred warriors.

Sadie saw that the arrowheads were being attached to the arrows, so the points were set at a right angle to the bowstring. This was so the arrowhead would pass between the enemies ribs. Hunting arrow tips were placed parallel with the bow string so they could pass between the buffalo ribs.

The feathers went on next, carefully glued in place

with the outside feather of a different color.

When a warrior went into battle or on a raid, he often carried a hundred arrows with him. Sadie knew that a Comanche warrior could keep an arrow in the air all the time as he shot them at a target from a running horse.

Black Bird tugged at her arm and at last the girls raced off, finding a dozen young dogs playing with a tiny squirrel. The girls screamed and bellowed at the dogs, running into their midst and sending them sailing every which way. They rescued the squirrel which promply bit Black Bird on the finger. She yelped and tossed the squirrel up a tree where it would be safe.

The other girls teased Black Bird as they raced back toward their lodge where Black Bird and Laughing Golden Hair settled down at their places and went back to pounding jerky into powder so it could be turned into pemmican.

Both the girls worked hard, watching each other. They knew they had a responsibility to help with the pemmican, so they settled down, chattering as they worked.

The next day the scouts came back. There were several herds of buffalo within a day's ride. They would strike camp and move out at once to get as close to the herd as possible for one last great hunt.

Moving the camp was always fine excitement for the children. The women had the most work to do. They packed everything into large rawhide boxes and skins, loaded it on a travois, took down the tipi, folded and rolled the large heavy leather cover into one large bundle and loaded it on another travois. Then made sure all of the twelve to fourteen twenty foot long tipi poles were tied on to another travois.

As the women did all this, the warriors circled the camp on their favorite war ponies, being always ready to defend the camp. Sadie figured that some of them could help, since there was no enemy coming after them. But it was the way of the People, and Laughing Golden Hair would not change it.

Some of the children rode travois, some ran along beside them. The older boys, and some of the girls, got to ride their own ponies. Sadie didn't have a pony yet, so she and Black Bird ran alongside for a while, then jumped on the travois bundles and tickled one another until they rolled off into the dust of the trail made by more than seven hundred horses and mules.

They camped late that night near a small stream. The warrior scouts said the buffalo were only a half mile away and not moving.

This hunt was to be different than the ones before. This area of the Staked Plains had sharp drops and some cliffs. The warriors planned not to kill the buffalo with arrows this time, but to let the shaggy beasts that ran as high as two thousand two hundred pounds, to simply kill themselves.

Sadie heard the talk but didn't understand it.

The next morning she did.

Almost a hundred warriors and older boys gathered in the woods along the river a half mile from their temporary camp and looked out at the area of brown backs.

White Eagle decided there were more than two hundred of the bison in this small herd. They were positioned almost where they wanted them. He sent ten warriors to the far side swinging wide around the herd so the animals wouldn't panic.

An hour after sunup, the Comanche warriors struck. They had formed a half circle around the near end of the buffs, and now rode at them, shouting and firing their pistols in the air. The bulls, roaming the outside of the herd saw the sudden danger and charged into the herd, scattering them a little bit but soon leading the entire sea of brown backs in a retreat, charging straight ahead away from danger.

When a shaggy old buffalo decides he's going to go in one direction, neither man, nor horse nor arrow can dissuade him. He's going that way, over river, trees, shacks, white man's cabins, anything that gets in the way.

The Comanche continued to chase the herd, firing the captured Pony Soldier pistols in the air, screeching their war cries, charging at laggards.

The herd plunged forward, crossed a small stream, went through a fringe of trees and a brush, crushing the growing things into the ground and grinding them up with sharp hooves.

When the first huge bison leading the charge sensed the danger, it was far too late. Directly ahead of their charge lay a fifty-foot cliff with a straight down drop off to rocks below.

The first buffalo tried to stop, but two hundred tons of charging bison behind them soon pushed them over the brink. More than a hundred of the shaggy beasts plunged to their deaths over the cliff before the less densely packed animals in the rear of the stampede turned and scattered each way.

The ten warriors on each side had little luck in turning them back to the dropoff.

White Eagle sat on his pony at the edge of the cliff. Below was the rest of the meat and a hundred new buffalo robes for his clan. He smiled and rode back to a trail that led down to the slaughter.

By the time he arrived two hundred women and girls were on hand dragging dead buffs off one another to an open space where they could be butchered. The horses and mules strained to pull the huge animals out of the pack. Soon the warriors used their war ponies to help pull the dead buffalo into the open for butchering.

That's when the real work began. The women and warriors both tore into the project. The buffalo meat had to be salvaged, butchered and cut into strips before dark, or it would be lost. For this reason the warriors condescended to help in the butchering. It was simply a necessity to save as much of the meat as possible.

If the drying process did not start the first day, there was almost no chance to save the rest of the meat.

Knives flew, drying racks were set up less than two hundred yards away to cut down the time it took to carry the meat to them. New racks had been made, but there weren't enough. More racks were improvised. Buffalo strips hung everywhere as the warm, smiling sun began the drying process.

No final skinning was done. The robes could be salvaged anytime during the next two or three days. Today was meat day.

When the sun at last slipped behind the edge of the horizon, the White Eagle camp members fell on the ground wherever they happened to be. They had not eaten except to gorge on the treasured raw delicacies as they butchered.

The men and women were blood stained from chin to ankle. They had more meat in racks than ever before, and if nothing went wrong, there should be enough for everyone, even the tipis where there was no hunter.

Warriors and women alike fell into the small stream and splashed away the blood and hair and smell of butchering from their tired bodies.

Then the women roused themselves enough to set meat to cooking over the fires. Huge slabs of meat were skewered on the back, and hung over cooking fires on tripods. A well moistened rawhide strip tied the skewer to the top of the tripod and eliminated any use of a skillet. The rawhide was wet often to keep it from burning. When the meat was done on one side it was turned over, skewered on the done side and tied again over the open fire to finish cooking.

That evening there were songs and games and eating and more eating. The buffalo meat that had not been dried would be good for two days. They would eat their fill now, then begin to work on the skins.

All of the animal was saved, the sinew from the spinal column was treasured for bow strings and strong cord for sewing together tipi covers. The stomach liners from the buffs would make cooking pots and water bottles. The brains were saved carefully to be used in tanning and preserving the hides and robes.

White Eagle walked among the carcasses of the mighty buffalo in the moonlight. He counted a hundred and twenty dead animals. They had saved most of the meat. It had been a highly successful hunt. To kill that many buffs with arrows would have taken three days.

White Eagle turned back to his quickly set up tipi.

It would be a good winter. There would be enough pemmican for all, and no one would starve. It would not be the winter the babies and old men cried.

He went inside his tipi and sat on the bed beside Slender Pecan. His hand felt of her flat belly and he scowled in the darkness. Then he took off his breechclout and lay on her. She welcomed him and spread her legs and whispered how she was going to conceive a son for him.

In the past weeks he had been hopeful, now he was anxious. He eased into her warmth and soon did his best, planting his seed in her. Now she must be fertile and conceive. He needed a son of his own. He would have a son to lead the band in the years to come. He must have a son.

5

A week later the White Eagle band's buffalo jerky was dried and stored in rawhide boxes, most of the buffalo hides had been scraped. The band would rest for another week or two, then began the last move of the season into their winter camp to the north with three other Comanche tribes.

Early in the summer four of the related Comanche tribes had decided to winter in the high reaches of the White River, where it flowed gently between two rising bluffs that would shield them from the fierce blue northers. The sturdy stand of live oak and pecan trees would give them a good supply of wood for their fires.

But for now White Eagle sat in his tipi with the flap closed, playing with little Danny. It wasn't manly to play with children, according to the Comanche way of thinking. But in the privacy of his own tent, White Eagle enjoyed the little ones, especially Danny since he was the only boy in his five child lodge.

As he played with the small white eye, White Eagle's mind was miles away. He had been nurturing a dream of vengeance for weeks. Ever since his camp had been attacked by the white eyes and so many killed.

He wanted desperately to drive the Pony Soldiers out of Comanche hunting grounds.

It would take a big effort, it would take most of the Comanches. But could he talk others into helping him? The Mesquite band would be the first. Tonight he would talk with the council here, convince them it was the only thing to do if the Comanche nation wished to survive. Another five years and they would be pushed all the way north into the lands of the Kiowa or the hated Tawakonis. Either way it would be a new enemy to fight just to try to find living space.

The Comanche nation once filled hunting grounds so vast you couldn't ride across them in seven sunsets!

Why should they let the Pony Soldiers take it away from them? Where the Pony Soldiers came, the white topped wagons soon followed with settlers, bringing plows or ranchers who brought in the white man's buffalo and ruined the ranges, driving away the one life giving staple of the Indian's existence, the glorious buffalo.

He would talk to the council tonight.

The warriors gathered around the council fire just as the western sky began to grow dark. The firelight bounced off the faces.

Each man was allowed to talk. There was no

"chief" as such, no man who had to be obeyed. The Comanche bands functioned as true democracies. Each man could speak, and each warrior was free to come to or go from any Comanche band whenever he wanted. If a new war leader was chosen, the old one could leave with as many loyal warriors as elected to go with him.

White Eagle sat in their midst and talked softly, yet firmly.

"We are losing our lands. Again and again we have been driven toward the setting sun. Even now we are in the very farthest fringes of our traditional hunting grounds, and who is to say that the Pony Soldiers will not find their way up here to the Stakes Plains?

They have pushed us away from our rivers and our plains, from the lands where the mighty buffalo roam and breed and raise new calves for our band to use.

"We must make a stand. It is my suggestion that we establish our homeland, our hunting grounds, the Comanche's living lands, once and for all. I suggest that we join forces with the rest of the Comanche bands and form a strong force and attack these forts where the Pony Soldiers sleep and guard their horses. If we burn down the forts, rout the soldiers and send them rushing back to their brothers to the east of Austin town, we will be the owners of our lands once more.

"Then it will be an easy task to rout out all of the settlers, all of the ranchers, all of those who bring in the scrawny white man's buffalo, and the terrible plows that kill Mother Earth's hair. We will smash them and burn them out and send any survivors flooding to the east.

"This is my plan, and my hope."

White Eagle waited for reaction. Generally it was as he had expected. His loyal followers supported him to a man. Most of the younger warriors were enthusiastic. Some of the older warriors who had come along with him because he always had good hunts and because his defense of his camps was good, were less sold on the plan.

"How do we know that we can rely on our cousins to support us in this battle?" Proud Buck asked. "We are only a hundred warriors. Each of the Pony Soldier Forts has at least twice that number. We would need four or five bands as large as ours to form a fighting force of five hundred warriors. How long would it take? How many forts are there we would attack?" He shook his head.

Proud Buck was the oldest warrior in White Eagle's band. He had more than fifty seasons, no one knew for sure.

"The more we talk about it the better," he went on. "We need to discuss it. The main problem is that it is too late this year to get the job done. No matter how good an idea, how good the plan, we are through with war for this year. Our pemmican is made or can be made, our jerky baskets are full. It is time for us to move into our winter camp and there battle the enemy who is ever staring into our tipis, the cold of winter, and the hunger of winter. I am finished."

One after another the top twelve warriors in the band had their say. When it was over, they seemed to agree. It was a mighty and a worthy project. They would have to go to war to solve their problems of territory. However, now was not the time, it was the time of fighting their oldest enemy, the cold and starvation of winter.

As was the custom, White Eagle had one last chance at the council.

"The council is wise and prudent in its talk about war with the whites. It must come sooner or later or we will die. That much is clear and we agree on it. I am convinced that you are right, now is not the time to strike. Now is the time to begin to prepare, to talk to our cousins, to the other fifteen to eighteen bands of Comanches and sound them out on conducting a total war against the whites.

"I will travel as far as I can before we move to our winter camp to contact others who will not be wintering with us. It is my hope that come spring, when our war ponies are strong again and eager to run, that we will be able to put together a force of two thousand warriors and attack and crush every fort on the setting sun side of Austin town."

Early the next morning, White Eagle and two warriors rode out to find any Comanche bands they could to talk to them about the great Comanche Spring War against the whites.

They rode hard for three days, down off the Stakes Plains to the north past the North Peace River, on above Mulberry Creek, and all the way to the Mighty Canadian River.

There they found the Sly Antelope band. It was a great congregation of tipis along the south side of the Canadian River and numbered almost two hundred.

Sly Antelope was a small man, but powerfully built and it was said there was no Comanche or Apache who would willingly face him in a knife fight. He had a slash on one cheek that drew down his left eyelid, but had not affected his sight.

Sly Antelope welcomed White Eagle and his warriors into his band with great fanfare, then listened to White Eagle's suggestion.

Sly Antelope spent five minutes telling White Eagle what an excellent plan it was, and how eventually the Comanche had to rise up and strike at the white eyes. Then he shook his head.

"Now is not the time, my cousin from the south. We have heard of your troubles with Captain Two Guns. We have heard how he scouted out your camp and fell on you without warning. We know of your sorrow and your anger and your loss.

"We also have heard about Laughing Golden Hair, and we say she is the heart of your trouble. If she had been killed in the raid there would have been no such trouble.

"We have not seen a Pony Soldier since before our winter camp last year. We are not bothered. I can't, in all good humor, take your proposal for an all out war with the Pony Soldiers to our council. They would laugh me out of the council fire."

White Eagle slumped where he sat next to the fire in the big tipi. It was larger, even, than his own.

"But you can see that the Pony Soldiers will eat us up one bite at a time if we don't band together. First the southern bands, then the middle and soon all of you up here on the Canadian will be the targets of the Pony Soldier's guns."

Sly Antelope looked at White Eagle, put a small log on the fire and sighed. "When I have a thorn in my foot, I stop running and take it out. When the thorn is in the trail two miles ahead of me, there's no sense in my stopping now and looking at my foot."

He stood and motioned to his wife. "We will eat now. There is nothing more to say about the big battle. It is not time for us here in the north to think about it yet."

There was nothing else White Eagle could do. The subject was closed. He visited the band for the rest of the day, and the next morning, he and his two warriors moved south toward the North Fork of the Red River where Sly Antelope said the Pecan Eater band was camped.

White Eagle and his men found the band shortly before nightfall that day and talked at once to Flying Hawk, the leader. He listened politely, said he had heard of the many Pony Soldier raids in the south.

"We also hear that you have irritated a Pony Soldier called Captain Two Guns," Flying Hawk said. "We have no trouble with the Pony Soldiers. It may be that you are in an area where the white eyes want to settle. We are sorry about that, but until the Pony Soldiers effect us more, our council will not agree to go three hundred miles south to fight."

They found Lone Bear and his band near Mulberry Creek, but much higher than where White Eagle had camped. Lone Bear was a distant relative and they stayed a whole day resting and eating before White Eagle brought up the purpose of the visit.

He talked quietly for fifteen minutes explaining the trouble they had with the Pony Soldiers.

Lone Bear called for more food when White Eagle had finished. They both ate the venison that had been roasted on the bone over an open fire. It was crisp on the outside but juicy and delicious inside by the bone. They wiped their greasy hands on their legs and grinned at each other.

"Cousin," Lone Bear said. "I would not try to tell

my cousin how to fight his battles. However on this one point I sympathize. Twice we have been chased by the Pony Soldiers from a different fort. Twice we have suffered dead. The Pony Soldiers are driving deeper into our territory as well. I agree with you that we must do something.

"But the time is too short. I can bring only sixty to seventy warriors to a running fight. If you have a hundred or a hundred and twenty, we still need another two hundred to raid one of the yellow stripe forts. We can talk in the spring. Now our band has one more hunt to make before the snow flies. We have much work to do yet in our fight with Mr. Winter."

White Eagle smiled softly. "But in the spring you will be with us. You will come together in a mighty force to help us rid the plains of the terrible disease that rides black war ponies and fight with bugles and wagons and long knives."

"Yes, cousin. You have my word as a Comanche, In the spring we will kill the Pony Soldiers and send them running back to Wichita Falls and Austin. Then we will do what we want with the settlers and ranchers on our hunting grounds."

When White Eagle rode back into his camp high on the Staked Plains, he was still not satisfied. The bands to the north simply would not help them, which left the six or seven bands below the Wichita River who might be persuaded. Only one other was a cousin, outside of those who would be in the winter camp. He would have plenty of time to talk to them in the snowbound months ahead.

Until then?

He sat in his tipi and pushed his hands under the soft buffalo robe. Slender Pecan grabbed his hand

and thrust it onto her belly. It felt different. He pushed back the robe and saw the slight swelling of her belly. He nuzzled it, patted it playfully and smiled at her.

"Your son has started his life and will be a visitor in our tipi in another six months," Slender Pecan said softly. She nuzzled his neck, then lay down. Before she had prayed that he would come to her every night, that he would use her fertile field for his seed and sew them as often as possible. She enticed him whenever possible.

Now it did not matter if he came to her or not. She was growing inside. She was bringing the leader of the band a son. She would be honored among his wives. And her son would some day be the leader of the White Eagle Band. She would name her son Prancing Eagle.

White Eagle did not visit his youngest wife that night. Instead he needed another English lesson. He went to Doris's bed and sat beside her.

"Pregnant," Doris said in English. "You must learn the English word for it. Pregnant."

When he understood what it meant, White Eagle said the world several times, then looked at her.

"You . . . pregnant?" he asked.

She laughed. "No."

"*Ka taikay,*" White Eagle said. "Don't cry, we try again." He pushed under the robe, slid his long body next to hers and found her naked and waiting for him.

Doris felt his hands on her and wondered if she would regret this some day. She wasn't sure. Right now it felt so right, and right now was when she had to do her living. Later would have to take care of itself.

By morning White Eagle had decided what he must do. He was determined to make one strike at the Pony Soldiers before the winter camp. He felt cheated out of his grand attack. Instead he would plan a smaller attack, one that would hold little risk, and would be a tremendous coup for him and a blow to the Pony Soldiers.

The following evening he talked to the council."

"We found no support for our fight with the Pony Soldier above the Wichita. They are not bothered by the Pony Soldiers. But below the Wichita River, Lone Bear and his clan will join us in the spring. We spoke only with his group. We will be able to draw enough support by the soft days of spring to launch our attack with more than four hundred mighty Comanche warriors ready to take many scalps."

He waited but there was no immediate comment. White Eagle went on. "I do propose a raid, one last one before the winter camp. A raid that will test the skill, the daring, the courage and the medicine of every warrior in our camp." He saw the heads of the warriors lift. He had caught their attention so he hurried on.

"I suggest a raid that will give the Pony Soldiers a black eye, that will deplete their resources and their ability to fight us. What I propose is that we stage a raid directly at the Pony Soldiers at the Fort below the North Llano River, the same one where Captain Two Guns hides in his tipi.

"We will come at them silently in the night. We will slip around their patrols and slip into the wire place where they keep two hundred horses. We will steal all of them. If we can't steal all, we will drive the rest out and scatter them across the plains. The Pony Soldiers will not even be able to chase us because we will have their horses."

"Yes!" a dozen voices shouted almost in unison. This was a raid they could understand. Each man on the raid could gain four or five sturdy horses. It was a risk worth taking, it was the traditional job of the Comanche warrior.

"We will leave as soon as we can get ready," White Eagle said. "We will need sixty of our finest warriors to go on this raid to come back with no scalps but many horses."

6

Eight days after the massacre of Lieutenant Edwards' patrol, the two Indina scouts returned from their trip. Hatchet came at once to the commander's office to report.

Major Harding had been talking with two of the new officers about various fort procedures. As soon as Hatchet came into his room, he dismissed the junior officers and as soon as they were gone, went to the big wall map.

"Show me where they went on the map," Major Harding barked.

Hatchet knew the map. He had worked on it before. He spotted the fort, then about the place where the patrol was killed. He saw a pin already there.

He traced a line almost due south from that into Mexico.

"Mexico, yes. Go there. Steal horses there."

"Then where did they go? Where are they camping?"

Hatchet's stumpy, dirty finger traced the map north from the ambush all the way to the southern end of the cap rock, then to the White River farther north. He stopped where the White River was shown coming out of the high rock escarpment that fronted what the Indians called the Staked Plains.

"They're camped up there on the White?"

Hatchet shook his head. "Not there. Go on up White into the high rocks, vanish."

Major Harding looked at him quickly. "I don't understand. The Comanche band isn't camping near the place where the White River comes out of the cap rock. Then where are they?"

"Up top. Went to Staked Plains."

"Goddamn!" Major Harding had never found a way up the steep walls to the top of the cap rock escarpment to reach the Staked Plains.

"So you think this bunch of Comanches has run all the way to the top of the Staked Plains. I didn't think the Comanche liked it up there."

"Not see other Comanche usual camp spots. Maybe many bands go up there."

Major Harding stared at the map. It was too far to go on a fishing trip. If he took a strike force four hundred miles he better have some good factual information to support it. He had none. He knew where the killer band had vanished to, but not where they were now. He also had no idea if this was the band he really wanted, White Eagle's bunch.

"Thanks, Hatchet. You'll get extra rations for your work." Colt walked the scout to the door, told Sergeant Swenson to arrange the extra rations for the two Indian scouts and went back to look at the map.

"Damnit!" Colt muttered. Four hundred miles up there and then not a clue where the murdering bastards went. Chances were the raiders were not even White Eagle's band.

He sat in his chair. That was one project out of the way. There would be no retaliation raid for the deaths of the seven troopers. It simply wasn't practical, too much work and cost for a possible retaliation. As the Fort Commander he had to reject the basic plan.

Hatchet said he figured the hostiles were on top of the high plateau. If so, did they take two hundred captured horses up there? How? Did Hatchet mean that the gorge the White River created was also a stairway up the cap rock to the Staked Plains? Possible. He'd keep that in mind in case the situation came up again.

What the hell now? He stared at the map again. Thousands of square miles where Sadie could be hidden. How the hell could he find her in two weeks? He'd have to get moving quickly. It would take another week here to get the fort running smoothly.

He had scheduled a training run with the Lightning patrol for nine o'clock, and it was almost time. Sergeant Swenson had his mount ready and by the porch when he came out.

Sergeant Casemore and Lieutenant Petroff were just bringing the company into formation as he swung on board his big black. He rode in front of the formation and Petroff snapped him a salute.

"Lightning Company all present and accounted for, sir!"

"Very well, lead the company out to the north of

the fort for three miles."

"Sir! Yes Sir!" Lieutenant Petroff replied, turned, gave the orders and the company swung into a column of fours and followed their commander out of the fort gate.

Once at the sight, the company put on a demonstration for Petroff showing him what they could do in picking up a downed trooper while riding at a gallop, and then moving off double. He seemed impressed. He watched as every man in the company rode by a target and swung off the saddle to the far side of his horse and fired at the target under the horse's neck.

"Jeeeeeeeeeeesus!" Lieutenant Petroff said with a display of true admiration. "They do that almost as well as the Apaches, and they're the best horsemen in the world. You trained them to do this?"

"Right, Petroff, and you're going to keep them sharp. They also get training in knife fighting from our Tonkawa scouts. They need more work with knives, and each man in the company is required to fire thirty rounds a week target practice."

Petroff looked up surprised.

"We don't list the rounds as fired at targets, Petroff. We put the expenditure down on patrol action against hostiles, and in defense of patrol against unseen attackers.

"I don't know if Phil Sparkman is fooled or not, and I don't give a damn as long as we get by with it. Whole damn Army should be doing it. The better marksmen we have the fewer rounds we need and the more effective our men are in a pitched battle."

"Agreed, sir. Agreed. There aren't many commanders who will follow through on that conviction. I'm pleased."

"Good. Today, Petroff, you are going to learn to do what you just saw your troops do. Two of the Tonkawa scouts will take you off a ways for practice. These scouts have been with me for two years. Trust them. The men will work one on one in mock knife fights. If we get in a hand to hand fight, I want these men to be able to use their knives and win against anybody."

By noon Petroff found he could swing off the saddle to one side or the other, fire under his mount's neck and not fall off. He hit the ground only once as he learned how. He'd have a bruised shoulder for a week.

They had no noon meal, and in the afternoon worked on tracking. Each man was required to give up his canteen before the tracking exercise. Only those who worked through the tracking problem and solved it got their canteens back before they reached the fort just in time for chow.

The men worked hard, but two were lagging. Harding took Petroff with him to question the two men. Both admitted they had lost their zest for the harder work this company had to put in. Both asked to be transferred back to their old regular cavalry companies.

As they rode away from the two men, Colt gave the new Lightning Commander a directive.

"I want you to open a competition on the post for men to join the Lightning Company. It will involve marksmanship, riding and physical exercises. The men who pass will be put on a waiting list for admission to the company to fill vacancies. Right now we need two new men.

"I'll set it up tomorrow, sir. Sounds like a great idea."

They rode back to the fort galloping half the way, then cooling the mounts out with a canter. Still each man had to spend a half hour rubbing down his horse and walking it to be sure the animals was entirely cooled out. Not a man among them grumbled. They had asked for this kind of duty. And they all knew any cavalryman was worthless without his horse.

Fifteen miles due west of the post, Captain Kenny led his twelve man patrol up a small water course and paused on a slight rise at the top. They could see for half a mile in every direction.

Lieutenant Schultz had performed well so far. He had looked frightened when they started out, but as the day wore on, he seemed to gain in confidence and in good spirits.

A startled rattlesnake suddenly struck at the horse just in front of Schultz as they passed through a rocky area. Schultz jerked his mount around the snake and galloped a hundred yards away from the line of march before he stopped.

Captain Kenny saw him go and followed. When the captain caught up with Schultz, he led the junior officer aside and they talked for ten minutes.

"Captain Kenny, I'm deathly afraid of snakes. Always have been and that . . . that was a rattler, right? Deadly."

"We tend to find them out here from time to time. Usually they're more afraid of us than we are of them. Only time a rattler will strike at a man or a horse, is when it's surprised and cornered or trapped or wounded and challenged. That's the first one I've seen in two months here."

"I'm sorry, sir. They still scare the hell out of me. I just go wild for a minute. I'll try to control it. I'm all right."

They continued the patrol, but Kenny watched the young officer more closely.

They had dismounted in a small fringe of trees along a tiny stream to eat a cold noon meal, when the man left on lookout reported a rider approaching. Schultz told Kenny he would check it out and went up where the lookout stood twenty yards away at the edge of the trees.

Ten minutes later the rider had come closer and suddenly three rifle shots blasted into the quiet afternoon.

"Indians!" Schultz bellowed. "Must be a dozen of them sneaking up on us." He ran into the small clearing by the side of the stream and huddled behind a tree. Half the patrol grabbed their rifles and ran to the edge of the woods.

Sergeant Franklin was the first one there. He looked out across the prairie and all he could see was a horse down and foundering about fifty yards off. A man huddled behind the mount.

"Chrissakes, don't shoot no more!" a voice called.

"Hold your fire!" Sergeant Franklin brayed.

The man on lookout shook his head. "Just a civilian riding this way, Sarge. I don't know why Lieutenant Schultz fired. There ain't no Indians out there."

Franklin said he'd take care of it and jogged out toward the horseman. The man stood up and stared down at his horse, then at Sergeant Franklin.

"You guys are Army? Why the hell you shoot my horse?"

"Mistake, sorry. One of our men got a little quick on the trigger. What you doing way to hell and gone out here?"

"Taking a short cut trail to Austin. Done it before from over in El Paso."

"Sorry, our mistake. Want me to put your horse out of his misery?"

The man shook his head, drew his revolver and shot the horse in the head. They took off the saddle, bridle and saddlebags and a small blanket roll and carried them back to the woods.

The man talked with Captain Kenny for a few minutes, then jumped up behind a trooper and they rode double heading back for Fort Comfort. His saddle and gear would be brought back at the end of the patrol.

Captain Kenny took Lieutenant Schultz upstream a ways and the men sat down by the peaceful flowing little creek.

"What happened, Schultz?"

"I swear to God that man looked like a Comanche brave sneaking up on us."

"Have you ever seen a Comanche warrior?"

"No, but I've seen pictures."

Captain Kenny threw a rock in the creek. "You said there was a dozen of them."

"I . . . I . . . don't know. I guess I just went crazy for a minute. There was just the one."

"Schultz, are you frightened?"

"No. Of course not . . ."

"I am," Captain Kenny said. "I get scared every time I leave the fort. It's natural. You wouldn't be human if you weren't a little frightened. It's what helps keep us alive out here. But it's something we have to learn to live with, to overcome. Do you think you can do that?"

"Of course. I'm an officer of the U.S. Army. I feel much better now. I don't want to hold up the patrol."

Before they started their ride again, Captain Kenny told his sergeant to take the rounds out of Schultz's rifle without his knowing it. He did.

The patrol continued. Captain Kenny assigned Sergeant Franklin to shadow Lieutenant Schultz, stay with him every step of the way and keep him out of trouble. Schultz made the ride the rest of the day, did what he needed to do, but was nearly paralyzed with fear.

Once he refused to lead the patrol through a narrow passage between two low hills.

"Hell no!" he bellowed. "That's a prime ambush spot. We should go around the left hand hill. I won't be responsible if we are forced to ride through that area."

Sergeant Franklin looked at Captain Kenny who nodded. Kenny led the patrol a mile out of its way around the small hill rather than upset Schultz even more.

Back in his office at Fort Comfort, Major Harding heard there was some problems with the settlers. He took his orderly and three troopers and rode down to the homesteads. All of the soddy houses were up and smoke was coming from chimneys.

The two ranchers had been on a roundup, using the farmer men as cowhands, and rounded up nearly fifty head of wild Texas cattle. They were in a rough pen bounded on one side by the creek's brush line, on another by a low draw, and on the third by a fence strung with smooth wire.

Major Harding saw Bert Banning working on the fence and he stopped by.

"See you rounded up some beef?"

"Damn right. Josh and me and the men pulled

them in over a three day roundup. Ain't they pretty?"

"Fine for now, but how you going to feed them when the grass freezes up and the snow flies?"

Bert took off his hat and rubbed his face with a rough hand.

"Way I figure it, Major, is that us folks here will be eating them critters. Then too, I had hopes of selling about two thirds of them to the fort for beefsteaks. Thought we might work out a trade for some staples, flour, sugar, potatoes maybe and some salt, even some tinned goods."

"Yes, Bert, I like the way you think. Why don't you start delivering one beef to us every Monday morning? Be a nice change of diet for the men."

"Sounds fair to me, Major. And congratulations on your promotion."

"Thank you. How are the houses working out?"

Bert laughed. "Womenfolk at first were thrilled to be in out of the wind and the chill. Now they're starting to make plans for bigger places, log houses or even frame houses. You know how womenfolk are. Told them we'd be in adobe block houses whether they liked it or not come next summer. Takes some getting used to. They still call adobe, 'mud.' Takes a damn lot of getting used to for some of these women."

The soldiers waved at him and rode to the next place. Henry Zigler came out of his soddy with a frown.

"Major. Just about to come up to the fort to see you. I've got a problem with the cavalry and the cavalry's got to do something about it."

"What's that, Mr. Zigler?"

"My eldest, Lucy, has got herself in a family way.

She tells me it's one of your lads from C Company. Don't ask me how or when it happened. Thought I was watching her fair. She's been the wild one in the family. Figure the army should discharge the lad so he can marry Lucy and settle down here on the farm."

"That's a problem, Mr. Zigler. Usually the Army can't discharge a man unless it's a criminal case. Tell you what. You bring the girl to my office this afternoon and we'll have her point out the man. We'll check his enlistment. If he's close to the end of his enlistment, we might make a compromise."

Zigler touched his hat brim and went back inside the soddy.

They talked with the others, then circled the area and went back to the fort.

Promptly at two p.m., Lucy Zigler and her father arrived at his office. Lucy was not much of a looker. She was firm and solid with big breasts and hips for easy childbirth. Lucy had stringy brown hair, a pout on her face and one eye that sagged a little, and she wasn't given to smiling much.

She wore probably what was her prettiest dress, a calico print that covered her chin to shoe tops.

"The man who done me is in first squad of C Company," she said softly. The ten men of first squad were brought into a line on the parade grounds. Lucy, not yet showing her family situation, walked down the line of men and then Major Harding talked to them quietly.

"Men, this lady says one of you has been familiar with her and she is now in a family way. It would be to the benefit of all concerned if the involved party would step forward so we can see what kind of just arrangements we can make. Please step forward now."

Two men took a step toward the major, saw each other and glared.

Lucy covered her face with her hand, laughing softly.

Henry Zigler scowled at his daughter and shrugged his shoulders at Major Harding. The two privates and the Ziglers went into the Major's office and all stood stiffly as he stared at them.

"It seems we have a problem here," Major Harding said. He turned to Lucy. "Both of these young men evidently were involved in a situation that could lead to your family way condition?"

She blushed now, but nodded, her face serious.

He turned to the men. "You both want to do the right thing and marry Lucy?" Both men nodded.

"You can't tell which one is the father?" Colt asked the girl growing weary of the affair.

"Lordy no, Major sir. I couldn't be rightly sure. They was both such nice boys and so close together."

"Then simply choose one, girl," Zigler said. "Let's get this over with. Which one do you want to wife with?"

She looked at both men, then went to the tallest, who seemed to be the youngest as well, and kissed his cheek.

"I want Lincoln," Lucy said.

Lincoln had another four months on his enlistment. He would serve out his time, be given leave from the fort every evening after five P.M. unless he was on patrol, and he would have Sunday leave. Josh Wilson, one of the homesteaders, had been a preacher early on. He would handle the marriage vows that very evening.

The Ziglers and their soon to be son-in-law hurried out of the major's office, and he went back to his paperwork.

Just before dark, a trooper was reported riding toward the fort by the lookout. Three men went to meet him, and escorted him to the major's office.

Private Longarm stood at ease in his commander's office. "That's about what happened, sir. I was ordered to tell you. The patrol is bringing in the rest of this gentleman's gear."

"Thank you, Private Longarm, you're dismissed. Report back to your company orderly."

Major Harding scowled for a minute, then told Sergeant Swenson to give the civilian quarters until the patrol returned. Then they should cut out an army mount to replace the killed one, and send the civilian on his way.

Swenson led the civilian out, and showed him where he could eat in the enlisted mess and gave him blankets and a bunk.

Major Harding mulled it over. Schultz. Colt had been worried about the man fitting in from the first moment he met him. Schultz had proved that he was not much good as a field officer. It might be just as well. So far he had caused the loss of only one horse.

On the last day of the Captain Kenny patrol, all was moving along well. They had completed their assigned sweep of a sector and were heading back to the fort.

Not a sign of an Indian had been seen. Lieutenant Schultz seemed to calm down, riding along and not paying much attention to what went on. He got through the two nights in his blankets near Captain Kenny without incident.

Now he was with the point man a hundred yards in front of the main party riding along confidently. They came to a small rise in the prairie, and suddenly, Schultz pulled the rifle from his boot and fired a shot ahead. There had been one round in the chamber of the Spencer. When he tried to push a new round in by working the lever, nothing happened.

Schultz dropped the rifle, drew his pistol and fired all five shots quickly at some unseen enemy to the front.

Corporal Nunes looked in astonishment at the officer. He could see nothing in front of them but the gently rolling Texas plains. When his pistol went dry, Schultz threw the weapon toward the front and wheeled his mount around and raced back toward the main party. Instead of stopping beside Captain Kenny he stormed past at a full gallop.

Sergeant Franklin dug his spurs into his mount's sides and whipped out after the lieutenant. It was over a hundred yards before he came up alongside the charging horse and could reach out and take the reins from the officer.

Herman Schultz stared straight ahead. His hands were frozen on the reins. Both horses came to a stop and with great effort, Franklin tore the reins away from the officer's grasping hands. They went to the saddle horn and froze there.

Franklin turned the officer's mount and walked both horses back to the main party, where Captain Kenny watched the affair with a frown.

Franklin led the lieutenant's horse all the way

back to the fort. Schultz had not said a word since he fired the shots. He stared straight ahead, but was breathing normally.

Some kind of shock, Captain Kenny decided. He had seen it during the war. A man's mind simply refused to undergo any more strain or fear, or terror, or the horror of combat with men's bodies flying apart and buddies dying in his arms. He'd seen it happen too often.

When the patrol arrived back at the Fort, Captain Kenny took Schultz directly to Doc Jenkins. Schultz would not talk, he stared straight ahead, but could walk and move, sit and lie down.

"Shock?" Captain Kenny asked.

"From what?" Doc asked. "You said it was an easy patrol, no hostiles, no problems."

"True. But horror can come in many forms. Just being this far from a big city could trigger it. The rattlesnake, maybe just the Texas prairie, and the memory of what happened to the last patrol we sent out."

"Maybe. I'll keep him here for a time. You tell the major."

Then Major Harding listened to what happened.

"I'm not really surprised, Captain. We might be lucky to catch it so quickly. At least we didn't lose a whole patrol or a company of troops because he lost his mind. We'll send Schultz back to San Antonio with the next courier run. There should be one in a week or two."

Just before mess call, two officers came to see their commander.

"Sir," First Lieutenant Jefferson said. "We're both here to request that our wives and families be transported from San Antonio to this post. We were told that this is not a hardship post, and that families are permitted. Colonel Sparkman asked us to look over the fort for a week or so and then decide."

The other officer was First Lieutenant George.

"Winter is no picnic out here," Major Harding said. "It would be a lot easier on your families if you could put off the move until spring."

"But, sir, I've got a two year old and a one year old," Franklin said. "I don't want to miss that much of their growing up time."

Major Harding nodded. He had been there himself. "Give me a week to think it over, then I'll make a recommendation to both of you."

"Being married, we both really miss our wives," George said.

Colt Harding winced and Lieutenant Jefferson hit Lieuteant George in the shoulder.

"Sorry, sir," George said. They hurried out of the room.

Colt stared out his small window. He was sure they missed their wives. He knew how that felt. The men would be more stable, better officers with their families here. He just wanted to be sure in his own mind that there would be no danger. He didn't want any more families subjected to the terror of an Indian attack.

He had a week to decide. Slowly Colt thought over the situation here at Fort Comfort. Things were meshing nicely. Lieutenant Petroff had been as good as Colt thought he would be with the Lightning Company. The men were pleased they had one of "their own" as their new company commander.

Lieutenant Schultz would be heading back to San Antonio soon. The other new officers were working out. The fort had settled back into a routine. It was time to make his plans to go bring back Sadie from White Eagle. He turned again and looked at the map of Western Texas.

7

In the Staked Plains camp of White Eagle, there had been talk of nothing else but the raid on Captain Two Guns's fort. It would be a dramatic coup just attacking the place, whether any scalps were taken or any horses stolen.

The honor, the daring. The good medicine it would generate for every warrior who participated in the attack would be tremendous. For a time there was wrangling about who would be allowed to go.

More than twenty young boys, aged fourteen and fifteen, pleaded to go along. They were turned down. It was far too dangerous to risk the young manhood of the entire band.

In the end, the council sat around the fire long into the night and made the final decisions. All fully qualified warriors were allowed to go, however certain of the older man were asked to stay and defend the camp. Not every warrior in a band went on a raid, since that would leave the women and children defenseless.

When it was all worked out, they found they would have seventy warriors on the trip. They would travel light and swiftly, living off the land or off a roll of pemmican. White Eagle decided that it was more than three days of hard riding to the fort where Captain Two Guns lived. A moment later he decided it would be four days hard riding, or perhaps five. He had never been all the way to the fort.

Near the fort they would take one full day to rest their horses and let them graze and drink to recuperate. Then they would attack at night under cover of darkness without fear of death since it was a quick raid. They would be there and gone before the Pony Soldiers could load their weapons.

Doris heard about the raid as soon as it was general knowledge. She had heard something about Captain Two Guns, but she could not remember what it was. A fort meant the cavalry and somehow she had to find a way to go along.

That night as White Eagle lay with her as they rested after a wild and furiously satisfying love-making, Doris asked if she could go along to cook for the warriors. He did not consider it for a moment.

"There can be no women along. If I take you, then every warrior will want to bring his favorite wife and we will be slowed down to fifty miles a day. We must move quickly, before and after the raid."

Doris rolled over on top of him. She had never done that before. She watched his face in the glow of the fire. At first he was surprised, then a small smile seeped into his face.

"This way? Let me show you something different."

A half hour later they rested again. He touched her nose and her eyes, then laughed softly. "You still can't go with me on the raid."

All the next day preparations for the raid continued. Runs Plenty was besieged by warriors for more arrows. He laughed at them, said they should have come a month ago. He continued working slowly and lovingly over each arrow that would spell silent death for man or animal.

His work could not be hurried. White Eagle told the warriors they would not need a hundred arrows for this raid. They would take their guns and perhaps not fire an arrow at all. Only the guards around the horses would be dispatched silently with arrows. Then, if everything went right, they would be gone before the sleepy white eyes got out of their wooden lodges.

Women shook out their best dresses, the ones carefully chewed into a luster and beaded with the bobbles from the traders. Those with elks teeth, strung them on their best dresses so each time they moved the teeth chattered together in a delightful sound.

Hair was braided anew, lances polished, war shields rubbed and bows readied.

As soon as the sun passed the midday mark, the drums began. Someone would beat the ceremonial drums until the last dancer fell in exhaustion sometime after midnight. The longer the dancers continued, the more good medicine it meant for their warriors.

When the sun dipped below the horizon, the great council fire was lighted and blazed up. The council members walked in and took their places, and the drums picked up in tempo. Now more than a dozen drummers beat out a rhythm that was different from the previous six hours.

This was the dancing beat. A line of dancers formed around the fire. The women and young girls dressed in their finest were on the inside, the men and older boys on the outside. They beat their hands or clapped as they shuffled around the circle, first one way, then when the drums changed beat, they reversed and went the other way.

At one point they moved so close to each other they almost touched. Suddenly the beat changed and they backed away and began to circle again. Each time they came toward each other it was a different man and woman.

The dancing continued for two hours. Some of the women dropped out. Others took their places.

Then a ringing, challenging Comanche war cry tore through the beating of the drums. From the edge of the firelight a warrior charged into the clearing on his war pony. He carried only his war lance, a fourteen-foot shaft with a shiny steel point.

Guiding the pony only with his knees and legs, he went around the dancers and skidded to a stop only a few feet from the council and dramatically flung his lance into a new buffalo skin which had been staked out on the ground near the council.

The warrior was Thunder Dog, one of the most skillful fighters in the band. He stood on his pony's back as the animal remained absolutely still.

Thunder Dog gave a ringing denunciation of Captain Two Guns and his gang of whites who were trying to take away the traditional hunting grounds of the Comanche nation.

"We will raid him. We will steal his horses. We will make him quake and tremble with fear of the mighty Comanche nation. We will return next summer and burn down his fort and drive him and his puny white men back to Austin town.

"We are Comanche! We are Comanche! We are Comanche! We cannot be beaten. We will be victorious on our raid, and we will return with many of the strong army horses to breed with our own fleet, sure-footed ponies, and we will live in the land of buffalo and honey and pecans for years on end, forever and ever."

Thunder Dog dropped onto his horse, and a great roar of approval went up from the three hundred voices of the White Eagle band. Thunder Dog rode his mount away, and the warriors who would go on the raid got to their feet and slowly circled the fire. The dancers gave way and sat around the edges of the firelight.

When all the warriors were assembled, there was another mighty cheer and the fighting men went to their buffalo robes and their women.

Then the dancers continued, the drums picked up and again the shuffling around the fire went on. Only older boys, older girls and warriors who were not going on the raid danced now. Slowly the pace picked up until one after another dancer gave way to fatigue.

It was just a little after midnight when the last couple sighed and collapsed in the dust. They were the strongest dancers in the camp, and would have the honor of leading the next dance, the victory dance when the warriors returned.

But for now they struggled to stand and stagger off to their tipi.

Doris lay on her low bed and watched White Eagle visit his two younger wives. He did not disturb Always Smiling, his oldest wife. She was already snoring away. Jealous? Doris laughed silently at the idea, then turned over and reached out to touch Danny to be sure he was safe and sleeping. Damn right she was jealous. White Eagle was an exciting lover who made her think and do the wildest things when they were making love. Even so she wished that she could go with him tomorrow morning, and slip away to freedom in that fort. She had to find a way to escape.

As she slipped off to sleep she wondered if now might not be the ideal time. Most of the best trackers and warriors would be gone on a raid. Yes. This would be a good time.

She would work on that in the morning. She knew only that they were on a high plateau and she would have to find the river that they had climbed up. Could she do that? She wondered if she could even find it as she drifted off to sleep.

The next morning Doris woke up as the camp stirred with the excitement of the raid. The warriors were up early. By daylight they rode out of the camp with fifty wellwishers cheering them on.

Doris was not with them. She had come awake as someone grabbed her right wrist. She was moved toward one of the tipi poles that came down forming the side of the tipi shell. Always Smiling tied Doris' wrist with a piece of rawhide. The knot was wet and when it dried there would be no chance it could be untied. The other end of the four foot long rawhide went around the tipi pole and was firmly tied with another wet knot.

"Stay here," Always Smiling said. Doris felt sick

to her stomach. White Eagle had expected her to try to escape, so he had left word for her to be tied up.

When the sun was up well, the knot was cut off at the tipi pole, and she was taken outside and tied to a stake driven deeply into the ground. They put a rock and hammer in front of her and she began making pemmican the way the rest of the women and girls did.

Now she felt like a slave. Laughing Golden Hair came up and began working beside her.

"They thought you would try to escape," Sadie said softly.

"They were right," Doris said. But now there was no chance at all.

The Comanche warriors rode only fifty miles a day so they would not wear out their ponies. It took them six days to get to the river they wanted and work down it so they could see the fort. Then for twenty-four hours they slept and let their horses rest. One patrol of Pony Soldiers came out from the fort, but bypassed the stretch of creek where they hid in the brush and woods.

The night of the eighth day on the raid, they waited until the sun went down, then judged their route and worked slowly toward the fort in the darkness. They expected a forward line of sentries around the fort, and had their best bowmen up front. However there were no such guards.

At slightly after midnight, they lay in the tall grass to the south of the fort. They were two hundred yards from the paddock where more than three hundred horses stamped and nickered and now and then bit each other.

White Eagle and two of his most trusted friends

dismounted and slid up to within touching distance of the wire on the posts. They had spotted the paddock guards. One stood at the far side of the pen next to the east end of the fort. The second one was near the gate which led from the paddock into the fort itself through the wide wall/building.

White Eagle had expected the white men to use wire. He had seen it before. On one of the ranches they raided they had to cut it and found that one of the white men's hatchets would cut the wire if it were first placed on another piece of iron.

Now he knew the noise would be too loud without some kind of covering sound. He whispered to one of his men who returned to the main party and brought up two hatchets they carried.

Another Indian went through the wire and among the horses. He jabbed one horse with his knife to bring a scream of pain from the animal and the accompanying wickering and horse talk among the other animals close by.

At the height of this noise, White Eagle cut the first wire next to one of the posts with two hard blows with the hatchet. On the third disturbance, the guard at the far end of the paddock came down along the fort wall to check the problem.

During the fourth cry of horses, the guard saw an Indian crouched among the mounts, but only for a moment before a knife flew through the air and sank deeply into his chest.

Thunder Dog rushed up, took the trooper's scalp and worked his way through the horses to the spot he had left White Eagle. Already thirty head of horses had been sent through the twenty-foot wide gate newly created between the two posts.

White Eagle and six other Comanches slid into

the paddock, leaped bareback aboard the mounts near the far corner and began driving the horses in front of them toward the gaping hole in the fence.

The guard near the gate into the fort called out in alarm. White Eagle rose up on a big bay and sent an arrow whispering into his chest, knocking him backwards, silencing his protest and killing him instantly.

They had more than half of the horses out of the paddock before a general alarm sounded. A sentry walking his post past the gate saw the paddock emptying, then noticed the dead guard and fired his rifle three times.

White Eagle gave an owl call and the men on horses inside the paddock slid off them and ran on the ground to the gate, out of sight between the rushing army mounts eager for freedom.

At the back side of the paddock the Comanche herders had formed the emerging animals into a group and began driving them north. They had brought up the war ponies of the six warriors in the paddock, and now all seventy Comanche worked the hundred and fifty horses to the north. Shots slammed through the night air behind them.

White Eagle could hear the angry commands as troopers were instructed to close the hole in the fence, then to catch a mount and saddle it and give pursuit.

White Eagle gave a shrill Comanche war cry and picked up the pace, driving the army mounts as fast as he could to the north and to safety.

Behind him Major Harding stood at the paddock swearing. He waited while Sergeant Swenson found a mount for him. He had heard of the problem almost at once, sent Swenson to alert Lightning Company, and put every man on the base on the alert.

Lightning Company was instructed to mount on any horse the men could find the form up for immediate action.

Captain Riddle ran up, buttoning his shirt.

"I just heard."

"How in hell could this happen? The damn Comanches right in our own paddock. They stole half of our mounts. We'll be the laughing stock of the whole damn army if we don't get back every damn one of those army paid for horses."

Swenson led up a saddled horse with a Spencer repeating rifle in the boot.

"All set, sir. Two hundred rounds in the saddle bags. Lieutenant Petroff has half the company ready."

Colt stepped on his mount and whirled away, walked through the mass of men and horses to where Petroff sat.

"Petroff. I'll take this half, you bring the rest of the Lightning Company when they're mounted. Tell Captain Riddle I want every man on the alert, every trooper possible to mount to ride under Captain Kenny to the north. We have to recapture every damn one of those mounts. Troopers! Forwarrrrrd Hoooooooo!"

Twenty men from the Lightning Company trotted out the front gate, then broke into a gallop heading north. They couldn't even hear the Comanches.

Major Harding rode the horses hard for a half mile, then dropped the gallop to a canter and began eating up the ground. Twice he saw Army mounts munching on late summer grass. When they crossed a small creek, there were a half dozen more. Good. The Comanche were having trouble herding them in the dark.

He pressed ahead. The Comanche would drive the horses hard, gallop them for an hour before they eased up. That would give them a head start. He had to close the gap.

After the first hour he would start to gain on them.

After three hours of cantering and galloping in a pattern designed to push the mounts to near the breaking point but never going over the edge, Major Harding pulled his troopers to a halt on a slight rise and listened.

Far ahead he could hear whoops and yells of the Indians as they herded the docile Army mounts.

"Gaining on the bastards!" he cried and they galloped forward again.

By Major Harding's pocket watch, it was four-thirty when they came on a pair of rear guards. The Indians had rifles but were not good shots. They fired, giving away their positions and a dozen rounds from the Lightning rifles spaced around the muzzle blasts killed both Comanches.

The Lightning Company men galloped again. As daylight broke in the east, they could see the Indians ahead, struggling now to maintain the herd. A few had straggled along the way, but Harding pressed on after the main party.

The Comanches saw them coming and sent back a delaying force of twenty men. The Indians were without any leader and bunched on the trail. Major Harding ordered his twenty troopers to space themselves out at twenty yard intervals and they simply rode through the Indians, killing three of them with accurate rifle fire. The remaining Comanches fled to the west.

Again Colt Harding closed in on the herd. The Army mounts were tiring, and more and more stragglers fell by the wayside, some foundering, some escaping and munching on grass or finding a stream for a drink. They would be easy to round up later.

The route north led past the Texas Colorado River. It had to be forded. A storm in the mountains two days before had sent a flood downstream that just arrived when the Comanche approached the usual fording spot that morning about seven A.M. An Indian charged into waters on his pony and was quickly swept downstream until he could struggle back out of the water on the same side.

White Eagle turned his catpured mounts upstream looking for a better ford.

Major Harding topped a small rise and saw the surging stream a half mile ahead, and the direction the Indians had moved the herd. He shifted his direction, angled across the route the Comanches had to take in an effort to cut them off.

He put the cavalry mounts into a gallop and kept them at it for ten minutes longer than he wanted to. He had utilized a dry water course and was out of sight of the savages. When he cantered his troops up to the edge of the Colórado he saw that he had beaten the Comanches. He positioned his men in the fringe of woods along the stream and waited. They let the lead horses and the Indian herders get thirty yards beyond them before they opened fire.

Six of the Comanche raiders went down dead in the first angry volley from the twenty-one Lightning rifles. Ten more Comanches saw the slaughter and wheeled back downstream. Fifty Army mounts slowed and stopped along the stream.

Major Harding moved his still mounted men downstream slowly, watching for the Indians. They worked through the pack of mounts who now settled down to drinking and eating. Some dropped to their knees. A few rolled over on their sides, in total exhaustion.

A flurry of shots sounded ahead of them. Major Harding feared the Indians might try to kill the horses if they couldn't steal them.

"Forward, charge!" he bellowed, and the twenty Lightning troopers spurred through the light brush and woods along the side of the stream. Two hundred yards below they found a dozen Comanches trying to shoot the horses. Six were dead already. The riflemen used their long guns and knocked two redmen off their ponies, and scattered the rest.

From the side, thirty Comanches stormed in to attack Major Harding. Just at that time the other twenty Lightning troopers under Lieutenant Petroff burst out of the woods from downstream and sent a volley into the charging Comanches. Five fell dead before they could turn and swarm to the left, away from the river.

They rode hard, leaving their prize, leaving their dead, intent only on getting away with their lives.

Both elements of the Lightning Company charged after them. The Comanches would ride their sleek Indian ponies to death to get a two mile advantage, and Harding knew it. He rushed after them for a mile, then sent a volley of army lead after them and pulled up.

"Lieutenant Petroff, you really know how to make an entrance," Major Harding said reaching out to shake his hand.

"Glad to be of service, Major. I'll get my troops busy rounding up this Army horseflesh."

Quickly Petroff established a holding area, put five men in charge of it and began driving in Army mounts one, two and three at a time.

An hour later Captain Kenny arrived with sixty men. They had rounded up twenty head so far from the stragglers, and were moving them back to the fort.

Major Harding went down to look at the dead mounts. He and Captain Kenny walked around the six dead horses and the five slain Comanches.

"Damned shame we lost six," Kenny said. He bent to look at a dead Comanche and the Indian surged upward with a six-gun aimed at Kenny's chest.

Major Harding drew one of his pearl handled .44's and sent two slugs into the wounded Comanche before he could pull the trigger. The rounds killed the Indian.

Major Harding kicked the other Indians, making sure they were dead before he put his gun away. The Indians and the dead horses were left where they lay. They had no tack or saddles to save. Major Harding did recover three pistols and one army rifle from the dead comanches.

A half hour later Petroff had the horses rounded up. He formed a team to drive the animals and began a slow trip back to the fort.

Petroff had put outriders stretching a mile each way to sweep the land for any Army mounts that might have wandered off. Most of them were too tired to go far.

They drove them three miles, and let them feed

and drink and rest for an hour. Then they moved another five miles and gave them another break. They could see the fort from there. Captain Kenny had a count on the horses his men had found and driven back, twenty-six. There had been three dead ones that foundered.

Major Harding did not want to estimate the number they had in their herd. They would be counted as they were sent into the paddock.

Nine horses dead. He wondered how many men had died in the raid? Two or three paddock guards, at least. He had lost no men from Lightning. Captain Kenny said he'd had no casualties.

"It could have been worse," Lieutenant Petroff said.

Major Harding looked up and growled. "It will be. Wait until I write up a report and sent it to Colonel Sparkman. He's going to chew us out for an hour."

They got back to the fort with the captured horses a little before three that afternoon. Already it had been a long day.

The official count of horses stolen was a hundred and forty-eight. Of that number six had been shot and killed by the Indians and three were run to death. A hundred and forty had been recovered and two were listed as missing.

"Those two missing nags will get hungry for some good oats and be back within three days," Petroff said.

He was wrong, it took the two mounts four days to walk into the fort, right through the main gate and head for the paddock. Both got a big muzzlebag of oats.

Major Harding found the two dead guards, wrote their next of kin and finished his report to Colonel

Sparkman. He wouldn't make the raid quite as serious as it had been. Listing the nine horses killed by the Indians and two guards dead.

It was the first instance of the Comanche Indians attacking an established post of the U.S. Cavalry in the Army's history.

Major Harding would just as soon not have had the honor of commanding the post the hostiles attacked. It wouldn't do him any good.

He thought of having Hatchet backtrack the Comanche, but decided not to. It would take another week and a half, and he didn't have that much time. Within the next two or three days he had to get his horseflesh in motion and go and find Sadie.

8

It took Fort Comfort two full days to settle down after the raid. Patrols went out more often, scoured the area around the fort with an intent thoroughness. Everyone was alert.

Captain Kenny suggested that interior guard posts should be added to the roof over the paddock area and over the north side as well. Major Harding agreed and the guard was increased by two posts and they were manned that same night.

The paddock fence was repaired, new horses assigned to those men who had lost their mounts among the nine dead.

One of the dead guards had been a Lightning Company man. He was replaced from the waiting list of men anxious to get into the Lightning group.

Major Harding finished his report on the affair, indicating that the attack evidently was in retaliation for some former campaign by the fort's personnel. He indicated the specifics of the death of the two privates. Then he pointed out that there had been no damange to the fort itself. The only other loss had been nine horses. The attackers were chased well into the north country. There was no chance to overtake and engage the enemy so the chase had been broken off.

He wasn't sure how Colonel Sparkman would react to the affair, but there was little any of them could do to protect the forts, ranches or small towns from such hit and run attacks if the Comanche were determined to make them.

Major Harding decided now was the time that he had to go try to rescue Sadie. If he didn't go in the next two or three days it would be too late. He wrote up orders for himself for three weeks of accumulated leave. He told the officers he was going to St. Louis to see his sister there and relax for a few days.

Only Captain Riddle knew the truth.

"You're going out again with your Indians?" Riddle asked him that afternoon.

"Yep. It's the only way we can get through the Comanche's network of lookouts and relatives to even find where they are holding Sadie. Finding her is going to be the toughest part of the job. You realize how big that land is out there? Three hundred by three hundred miles, give or take a dozen. We might look for three weeks and not find a trace of White Eagle's camp. Who can tell?"

"You know you're going with six against two or three hundred Comanches. Their women can be as tough as their warriors. Don't try to take a knife away from an old squaw."

"I just want to grab Sadie and run like hell,

preferably on a couple of good horses."

"I wish you well, Colt. I'll hold down things here with the usual patrols. Had thought of going on some longer runs now that the hostiles will be pulling back into winter camps. We can talk about it when you get back."

"With Sadie," Colt added.

He left the next morning, early, riding out on a sturdy Army mount with saddle, but with only saddlebags, a blanket and a little salt and beef jerky. He wore buckskins, a slouch hat, and carried his spencer and both pearl handled six-guns. They stirred no surprise from the gate guard. Weapons were needed for a trip anywhere in the West, especially from there to Austin.

He rode down a half mile, out of sight of the fort and turned into the brush along the river. Hatchet and five of his best trackers waited there.

Only Hatchet had a saddle on his horse. The other had their Indian ponies with a simple surcingle and army leather bridles. They wore only their breechclouts. Hatchet had on a worn, blue shirt.

Colt had promised each of them a double eagle for the trip. He had given each an eagle coin worth ten dollars the day before. When they got back each would get another. It was three times what the army paid them a month as scouts.

They turned north and rode hard for the first four hours. They came to a known camping area the Comanches once used, but there was no sign any Indians had been there recently. They pushed on north until after dark and shared a roasted rabbit over the fire.

Colt had not expected to find anything close to the fort, but he had to check out the possibilities.

Midway through the afternoon of the second day they touched on two other regular camping areas of the Comanche along small streams where there was plenty of grazing for their horses, but no Indians were there.

Nearing darkness they approached a site on the banks of the Colorado River known to be used. This time they found tipis, about twenty strung along the shore, but there was no large tipi with an eagle painted on it.

It wasn't White Eagle's band, so they went around it without letting the Comanches know they had visitors.

Two days later they found another camp, this in the fringes of the small hills below the Double Mountain Fork of the Brazos. There were nearly fifty tipis. It could be paydirt.

Colt and Hatchet worked up silently as death through the fringes of brush and trees until they could look down forty yards on the first of the tipis. None of them seemed to have an Eagle on it, but some could not be seen clearly.

They watched until darkness came but saw no evidence of any captives, women or children. With darkness they worked closer and along the length of the camp. At last they were certain. This was not White Eagle's band.

They moved far enough away to make camp and start a fire. Two of the Tonkawas had brought down a dear and they feasted on venison all that evening and half the morning. They ate as much of it as they could, wishing they had some way to preserve it.

If it had been cold enough they could have taken along a quarter of the venison and let it freeze, then cut off what they needed each day.

That afternoon they began riding east along one of the rivers, looking for camp spots. Now they had to zig-zag to cover the best possible watering places for the Comanches. Twice they almost blundered into Comanche camps. Both of them were small and couldn't have been White Eagle's band.

They worked slower after that, moving east, then back west almost to the cap rock, then east again.

The sixth day they came to White River and worked along it to the soaring rock wall that protected the Staked Plains.

"Where did you say those tracks vanished?" Colt asked Hatchet. The Indian rode ahead another quarter of a mile and pointed to a thin slice through the granite walls that seemed to go all the way to the top.

"There, all vanish," Hatchet said.

Colt studied where the rushing stream burst from the rocks and moved into the plains. There was a gorge of sorts, but it didn't look like it went far. They rode up to it and looked in, then Hatchet rode into the foot deep stream and waded to the entrance. He motioned Colt forward.

The opening behind the entrance was larger, with some dry areas and a rocky ledge. They could see that the power of the water over the centuries that had worn down the rocks, eventually digging a path all the way to the floor of the plains. He wondered if at one time it was a waterfall over the very lip of the cap rocks above.

"How far does it go in?" Colt asked.

Hatchet shrugged.

"Let's go find out." Colt led the way, wading his mount through the opening and into the gorge itself. From this better vantage point he saw that the gorge did not go straight back, it curved and as it did it slanted upward. The whole thing looked more like a series of steps and waterfalls than a canyon.

On the dry shore he found hoofprints.

"Damn, somebody did come this way," Colt bellowed over the sound of the rushing water. "Wonder if they got all the way to the top?"

"Let's go," Hatchet said picking up words and phrases quickly. Colt grinned and the white man and his six Tonkawa guides began to work up the water course, over the shoals and the rocky ledges. At the first ten-foot waterfall they stopped, then found a path around one side where the water had carved down more of the cliff during a high water time.

More hoof prints.

"Somebody rode up here," Colt shouted. They all worked carefully up the bank, around the rocks, through the water and up another slope. An hour later they were halfway up the gorge. It was as if the water had cut a series of small steps up the cliff and over the ages wore them down into chunks that could be mastered by a horse.

Higher up they came to a canyon that cut into the main gorge from the left. It looked less steep and it was dry. A short way up the dry arroyo they found more hoofprints. Soon Colt realized the gorge would take them all the way up. He grinned.

When they got to the top, they looked out with suspicion, not knowing what they might find.

It was flat, perfectly flat like some giant knife had sliced off half the world and left this table top. It was washed with brown waving grass. Far off to the north they saw a band of green ribbon in the brown.

"A stream up there, with trees. Must be a lot like

the rest of Texas. Let's take a look at it."

They rode forward and found the trees little more than a mile away. Coming up to the trees, they could see no indication of anyone living on the Staked Plains. Miles and miles of prairie, waving grass, now brown and dying, a few ribbons of green near what must be streams.

Far off to the north, Colt saw what he thought might be mountains, but the longer he looked, the more he decided he was looking at layers of clouds. There were no smokes, no animals, no Indians.

"If they came up here, where the hell are they?" Colt asked.

They decided it would be best to wait until darkness to move out and continue their exploring. That would be far better than running into a hundred Comanche warriors with their bows strung.

One Tonkawa took the watch while the rest of them stretched out in the grass and slept. The Indians dozed off at once. Colt found it hard even to shut his eyes. He couldn't sleep. When dusk fell he roused the others and they mounted.

They had worked silently up the stream for a mile when Hatchet held up his hand to stop. His nose quivered. Then Colt smelled it.

"Smoke," he waid. "A wood fire somewhere close by. Which way, Hatchet?"

The short Indian turned slowly, then pointed to the north. They came out of the trees, welcomed a scattering of clouds over a half moon, and rode softly toward the smoke smell. A quarter a mile north they came to clumps of trees, some pecans, and live oaks. Through these they found a gentle down slope and at the bottom of it the darker green of trees and what must be a river.

Now they could see the smoke, hear voices. They left their horses and slipped up on foot.

From behind a big live oak tree, Colt stared at a Comanche band holding some kind of a dance. He counted twenty-five tipis. It was too small a band for White Eagle, unless his had been split up by internal strife.

He waved the Tonkawas back and shook his head. "Not White Eagle's band," he whispered. They circled around the group and followed the river downstream. It meandered all over the nearly flat surface of the Staked Plains. Again they smelled smoke and then another.

Before Hatchet was through pointing out smokes, Colt decided that his nose must be crazy. The chief scout had indicated that wood fire smoke came at him from three different directions.

"Is your nose drunk?" Colt asked.

Hatchet grinned. He was known to lift a bottle of beer or two when the chance came.

"No drunk. Many smokes."

"We wait until morning and find out what we stumbled into," Colt said.

They tried to sleep. Colt was tired. He had grown used to the rough rides, the long hours, the physical exertion of the camping and cooking out. But somehow he couldn't sleep. He had a feeling he was close to Sadie, and nothing was going to stop him from rescuing her. Nothing.

He dozed off now and then, but woke with a start each time. The dream was always the same: some wild eyed, long haired, painted Indian warrior was about to hurt Sadie. Colt screamed at him and charged, running as hard as he could but just about the time he got there, the warrior turned into

Colonel Phil Sparkman who was berating him for taking unauthorized leave in the middle of a serious Indian rebellion.

Colt wiped sweat off his forehead and stared into the darkness. It was no lighter out. He didn't want to risk a sulphur match to check the time. Clouds covered the Big Dipper so he couldn't use the cowboy's way of telling star time.

He sat up and cleaned the bore of his Spencer rifle by feel. He wondered if he could take the Spencer apart and clean and oil it and put it back together again in the dark. It would be something for the men to practice. The better they knew their rifles and pistols, the better they would help protect their lives, and win battles.

Something moved near him. The shadow moved again and Colt's knife with a sharp six-inch blade slid from the leather home and pointed at the shadow.

"Hatchet!" a voice said, and Colt recognized his head scout. He relaxed.

"You no sleep," Hatchet said.

"Yeah. Right. Sadie is out there. I know it. I can feel it!"

"Many Comanches out there, too," Hatchet said. Then he moved away, curled up and went to sleep.

When morning came, Colt had dropped off to sleep. Hatchet touched his shoulder and sprang back. Colt came awake with his six-gun in his hand. He blinked, saw Hatchet and relaxed.

Together they crawled a dozen feet forward and looked out from the edge of the trees. They were on the side of a gentle bowl in the flat land, with a river running through below. Directly in front of them was a small camp of maybe thirty tipis. To the left they saw another bunch of tipi tops but could not say how many were there.

Far to the front were forty or fifty cooking fires warming up. Colt guessed the far camp could be five miles away, but sent volumes of cooking fire smokes straight up into the quiet air.

Hatchet motioned to Colt and they looked on the other side of the stream. Less than two hundred yards away they saw another Indian camp. The tipis looked like Comanche. There were twenty or twenty-five of them, and no painted eagle.

"Looks like we found where all the damned Comanches went," Colt said. "Let's move upstream and see if we can get a little cushion of space between us and those grave robbers out there. I'm not anxious to be the target for some wild-assed bow and arrow shooters."

They caught their horses, held their muzzles so they would not horse-talk with any nearby Indian ponies, and silently led the animals to the west through the trees and brush. They made it a half mile from the nearest camp, then relaxed for a minute.

Hatchet called Colt again and he looked out to the north.

Three Comanche warriors trotted toward their river. Each carried a bow and one arrow in his left hand, and a quiver of hunting arrows on his back. The trio was out after some early morning game.

Colt held himself still by willpower alone as the three Comanches came straight toward their position. One of the hunters shook his head and pointed to a different spot. The other two argued, then turned and angled into the woods a hundred yards below Colt and began working downstream.

Hatchet stared at Colt's buckskin shirt and shook his head. The head scout had long since discarded his shirt. Now he was unhappy with Colt.

"Take off shirt, hat," the scout said. "Look like Indian."

Colt got the idea. "So if the Comanche do spot us, they'll think we're seven warriors from another band? Yeah, good thinking."

Colt stripped off his shirt and was aware of his pale skin. They stowed the shirt and hat in Colt's small satchel, then Hatchet found brown clay and rubbed it into Colt's skin until he was nearly the same shade as the Indians. He took a length of cloth from Colt's pack and tied it around Colt's head to form a headband. From a distance it would help. Colt rubbed his face with the clay, and when he felt thoroughly filthy dirty, Hatchet nodded.

They worked upstream for another mile, then decided to wait for darkness. Colt was anxious to check out the far camp that had so many cooking fires. It could be White Eagle.

As soon as dusk settled over the Staked Plains, the six men got on horses and walked them slowly across the prairie toward the many smokes. Hatchet went first with Colt slumped on his horse next. Most of a man's height is in his legs, not his torso, so on horseback Colt did not look that much taller than the Tonkawas.

They passed within three hundred yards of the first village but no one even looked up. Further on, they moved through a small brushy area, then came to an open space a quarter of a mile across. The big camp lay just on the other side.

The six horsemen paused. It would be dangerous for the six of them to ride into the camp, or even close enough to see if there was a white eagle painted on the biggest tipi.

Colt moved up beside Hatchet and whispered a moment, then they circled the camp, moving off at a faster pace, rounded the far end and found a heavy growth of live oaks extending up the hill from the stream.

Without a word the men swung that way and were soon lost in the darkness of the live oak thicket.

They moved down closer, within fifty yards of the tipis and worked slowly downstream to watch for one tipi with an eagle painted on it.

Colt sensed sweat break out on is forehead. He felt so close to Sadie. This must be the camp.

They spotted one larger tipi but couldn't tell if anything was painted on it. For almost two hours they scouted along the fringes of the camp.

There was no way to be sure, it was simply too dark.

Hatchet suggested they move over the top of the small rise, find another creek a mile away and make a camp. They could hunt the next morning when it was safe. He would slip back into the woods and find out for sure if it was White Eagle's camp.

Colt Harding agreed.

"Damnit! This means another day. I wanted to get Sadie tonight." He sighed. "You're right, Hatchet. Good planning. This is one time we can't mess up or we'll all be dead. Right, let's move back and find a hidden camp somewhere. There might not be as many damned Comanches on the other side of the ridge."

It took them two hours to find the perfect hidden camp. It was in a low place a mile north of the big Comanche camp, and near no other camp. A thick stand of pecans hid them completely unless a hunter came directly into the thicket. There was room for their horses and at once two of the Tonkawas went out with their bows to find a late supper.

They would not make a fire until they needed one to cook. The night was crisp but not yet winter.

Colt Harding sat near his horse on his blanket, arms around his knees as he thought about Sadie. He had been at Fort Comfort for almost a year before he had sent for Connie and the kids. Sadie had been past three when he said goodbye to her at San Antonio. Now she was more than five.

Would he know her? More important, would she remember him? Those had been good days in San Antonio before he was assigned to Fort Comfort. His family was with him. Connie was a perfect wife. He told her she would be a general's lady someday—if he could toe the mark for another ten years. She believed him. Now that part didn't matter so much.

Christ but he missed her! She had been half of his life, Connie and the kids, now that was gone. Most of it. The part that was left was what he was fighting for now. And he *would* fight.

He went to where Hatchet sat.

"Could I slip into their camp and check it out tonight? I could make sure about that big tipi we saw, and come back and tell you."

Hatchet slowly shook his head. "Too tall. Comanche not dumb, somebody see you, put two arrows through you. All done. Better wait."

Colt knew he was right. It had been worth one last try. He stretched out on his blanket, then rolled up in it with one of his .44's in his right hand. Maybe now he could get some sleep. He knew damned well that this was the right camp. But now that they were here, they had to do it right.

Plan out his whole operation. First recon, to make sure of the target. Then observation, at least a day to try to find Sadie and tie down any habit patterns of the savages. Then plan the silent approach, how to get inside the tipi, find Sadie and get away.

The most important part was getting away. He figured they had to charge straight to the White River Canyon and get down it. If they didn't White Eagle would send men there first to cut off their escape. Then they would be trapped on the vastness of the great Staked Plains.

The infiltration had to be quick, clean, and they needed as many hours head start as possible.

Major Colt Harding kept working over the plan as he slipped off to sleep. It would work. It had to work.

9

Colt woke up slowly. It was just starting to get light in the east. Whatever was cooking smelled good. He found some salt from his kit and went to the coals where two rabbits roasted over the heat. It was a small fire, with almost no smoke. The Tonks had used dry wood. The drier the wood the less smoke it produced.

When the rabbits were cooked, the men tore them apart with their hands and ate the meat, licking off the bones. Colt finished the meal with two sticks of tough chewing jerky and a long drink of water.

He could not think about elaborate displays of delicious food. Later. He nudged Hatchet and together they worked back through the brush and wooded parts to where they at last lay in the pecans and live oaks above the big campsite.

Activity was beginning below in the Comanche

camp. Colt had brought his binoculars along, and lifted them, studying the camp. They slipped silently as two ghosts through the woods halfway down the length of the camp. The big tipi was directly ahead of them.

Colt lifted the glasses, moved twenty feet to his left and nodded slowly.

"A painted eagle on the big tipi. This is the White Eagle band." He said it so softly Hatchet asked him to say it again. Then they both grinned.

They lay in their concealed position for the rest of the morning, watching the activity around the big tipi. Many people came in and out the front of it. They could not see the flap.

Colt rested his eyes a minute, then looked again through the glasses.

"What the hell?"

Doris had just come through the flap and stepped to one side into the sun. Her white skin contrasted sharply with the Indians' skin. In her arms she held a nude two or three year old boy who was as white as she. He wiggled in her arms and she let him down.

"White woman and a kid down there," Colt said. He gave the glasses to Hatchet who had learned to use them. He grunted.

"White woman."

"Where the hell did she come from?"

Three little girls ran into the tipi and Colt caught a flash of golden hair. Had it been Sadie? It had to be Sadie. Comanches didn't have many blondes. He said nothing but pressed the glasses harder against his eyes.

A moment later the girls rushed out. The woman evidently called to them. They stopped and one of the little girls was blonde. She turned and talked to the white woman.

"Sadie!" Colt whispered. "It's Sadie! I see her down there. My little girl is right down there."

Hatchet had to put his hand on Colt's arm to remind him to be quiet. They were fifty yards away, but sounds carried well in the crisp Texas air.

Sadie ran between the tipis and was gone from sight.

Colt sat up and wiped sweat from his forehead.

"She's there. She's well and looks in good health. Christ, I've found my little Sadie!"

"We watch," Hatchet said.

Colt laughed quietly. "Yeah, Hatchet. Thanks for the reminding. You're the scout, I'm supposed to make the decisions. Right. We watch. Recon. We have to know if she sleeps there, or if she's just visiting. We have to know if they put out scouts. We have to know a damn lot of things."

Hatchet pointed to certain items below. There were well worn paths through the grass around the tipis. The dogs had scratched up resting places under the trees and next to the tipis. The herd of ponies at the far end of the camp had shown a lot of droppings. He pointed this all out to Colt who nodded.

"The camp here long time. Women start packing," Hatchet said. Colt could see the rawhide boxes being filled with items.

"Moving to their winter camp?" Colt asked.

"Two or three days more, then move," Hatchet said.

"So we have to find out everything we need to know today and tomorrow, and then go in tomorrow night," Colt said. It would take two days to recon to be sure what they saw was the normal way of operation.

Christ! They had almost been too late. He sent Hatchet back to their camp to take two of the Tonks to a place where they could watch the pony herd. It would be their job to slip in and steal two good ponies as Hatchet and Colt were grabbing Sadie and the white woman and her son. Three instead of one. It might cause some problems, but there was no chance that he could rescue Sadie and not the other two.

By the end of that first long day and evening, Colt knew the routine in White Eagle's camp. He had watched the tall Indian leader come and go from his tipi. He saw him greet a delegation from another camp. Colt had seen the warrior's shield, lance and bow placed precisely in front of the tipi.

And Sadie? For an hour he watched her play with two small Indian girls outside the tipi. It was a kind of game and she seemed totally at ease, not a captive. That could only mean that Sadie had been adopted by the Comanches, that they intended to make her into a Comanche and keep her forever.

"No!" he grumbled out loud. Sadie belonged with him. He hadn't even thought how he would care for a small girl child on an Army base, but there would be a way. First he would rescue her and the other two, then work on the next problem.

Colt had not been able to find any guards or security around the camp whatsoever. Were they so sure of themselves they did not have out any sentries at all? It looked that way.

There were plenty of warriors around. They did not work in the camp. The women worked hard on flat places where they could stake down what he guessed were buffalo hides. They were scraping some, applying some sort of fluid to others, tanning liquids he guessed. The sun did most of the work.

Sadie scraped on the hides from time to time, but the children seemed to run freely with little control. Whenever Sadie was in view, he could look at nothing else. How she had grown! Her blonde hair was braided down each side, evidently so she would look more like an Indian. She wore only a breechclout and seemed perfectly at home that way. Her fair skin had tanned and browned until she was almost the same shade as the other little girls.

Sadie always had been a happy little girl, quick to adapt to new things, new places. They had lived at three different army posts the first three years of her life.

As near as Colt could tell, White Eagle's tipi was home to little Sadie. She came and went from the big tipi, and the last thing before it got dark, he saw her go into the tipi and not come out. That was the spot they had to raid to get Sadie out, and right out from under the nose of the Great White Eagle, of the dreaded Comanche. It wouldn't be easy.

Hatchet came back just after dark. The ponies would be no problem. They were in a small, natural clearing surrounded by trees. The boys herding the horses had tied long strips of rawhide through the trees to form a kind of fence. That let the boys play in the stream and work at their bow and arrow practice and war games.

Hatchet nodded.

"Night, one, maybe two boys. We steal two horses, they never know."

"Good. It must be that way. We want to have three or four hours head start before White Eagle knows the captives are missing."

When the last activity around the camp stopped, and only the dogs ran up and down the areas between the tipis, Colt and Hatchet gave up and went back to their small camp.

One of their hunters had brought in a half grown yearling deer. The meat was tender and delicious. They roasted it a piece at a time and had a fire going for three hours before the men were filled. They slid the remaining good portions of the buck into the creek to cool so they would not spoil over night.

The next day they would feast again while the meat was still fresh.

Colt had the plan worked down, honed and refined and sharpened again. He laid it out for Hatchet, who nodded, made a change or two. Colt had wanted to cut through the back of the tipi and go in that way.

Hatchet shook his head. "Tipi cover much hard, tough, thick as fingers," he said. "Better go in flap. I go first, stop anyone who wakes."

"Quietly," Colt admonished. "We've got to be so quiet doing all this that nobody in the tipi wakes up. Sadie is staying in the chief's tent, White Eagle."

"If they wake, they dead," Hatchet said with a happy glint in his eye. "Comanche enemy!"

"Yes, I know. But quietly. Knife. I'll take Sadie and lead the white woman. You carry the little boy, and we hurry right back up here. The horses should be here by then and we'll haul ass straight for the White River Gorge that has that stairway down to the flatland."

They talked it over for an hour, then decided that the warriors with the horses should bring them to within twenty yards of the back of the tipis, so they would have less distance to run once they left the big lodge.

They stirred the coals and roasted more venison and ate again. It could be two days before they had time to eat after this time.

That night one of the Tonkawa braves stood guard over the small camp. Colt was not going to let any Comanche hunter stumble on them now and spoil everything.

They ate again in the morning, then put out the fire, cleaned up their small camp so not even an Indian would know it had been there and moved back through the woods to watch the Comanches.

There were no changes to be made in their plans. Now more and more large rawhide boxes were being packed with goods. The move would come shortly.

For one whole hour, Colt had the binoculars to his eyes watching Sadie and two small Indian girls playing. They went from the hides to a game of tag, then hit a strange ball with sticks through the grass and at last splashed in the water of the stream.

He couldn't wait to hold her in his arms again, to tell her how much he loved her and that he would always protect her. Little girls were something special to Colt Harding.

The hours dragged. Even Colt could tell that the Comanche camp was getting ready for a major move. By darkness all the skins that had been drying and being worked on had been taken up and packed away. The move was close, perhaps even the next day.

For an hour he talked with Hatchet about a diversion. A forest fire, or a flood. At last they decided they could do nothing that would not endanger the people and cause them to be alert too soon.

"What about their horses?" Colt asked. "I wish

we could stampede their mounts and chase them eight or ten miles out onto the plains."

"Then the Comanche know something wrong, find child and woman gone."

Colt nodded. He had been working on this for some time. "What if we leave two of your men behind waiting at the horses. When the camp stirs and they discover the captives missing, *then* stampede the horses and your men charge along behind them to cover our tracks and to get to the ravine gone down."

"Danger!" Hatchet said sitting up, looking angry. "Men get caught by Comanche. Two Tonkawas against three hundred Comanche warriors."

"You always say how you're better than the Comanches," Colt chided.

"True, but not three hundred against two."

"The Comanches will never catch them. They won't have their war ponies."

"Enough will catch ponies. Too hard to chase away six hundred ponies."

Colt saw a quiver around Hatchet's mouth. The idea interested him even as he talked against it. There had to be some way to convince him now that he was weakening.

Colt knew what it was. He shut his eyes a moment. It was the only way. This was war between savages. It had nothing to do with him.

"There might be a way to urge them to do the job," Colt said. "Let's say that four of your men stay behind to stampede and drive away the ponies. There are two guards at the pasture where the herd is."

Hatchet shook his head. "Four men, not enough."

"After they have stampeded the horses, and after

we all get safely down to the low prairie and away clean, there would be time for Comanche soup."

Hatchet looked up quickly. He grinned. Then he held out his hand as he had learned to do.

"Handshake bargain," he said, and scurried away in the late afternoon to tell his men how they would earn much money on this trip, help the small one escape, and still wind up having Comanche soup.

Colt lifted his brows. There was no other way. If the Comanches discovered the missing captives even an hour after they left, the swift little Indian ponies would overtake them before they could get to the White River Gorge and they all would die in a rain of arrows and hot lead.

They needed four hours and then the stampeded horses. Colt Harding didn't invent cannibalism. The Tonkawas were called the People Eaters by the neighboring tribes for good reason. It was a problem between the tribes. Colt was only using it as a means to an end. In this case the lives of three white captives weighed a lot more on the scales of justice than one Comanche herder. Dead was dead, what happened after that was of no concern of the victim.

Colt worked his way back to their horses and had a long drink of water from his canteen. He would keep on telling himself that setting up "soup" for the Tonkawas was the only way he could be successful in rescuing Sadie and the other two whites.

The Tonkawa scouts came in a short time later, laughing and talking softly among themselves. They watched Colt and nodded, then said the one English word they all knew, "good!"

Everyone but Hatchet laid down for some sleep. They would ride without sleep for the next sixteen or eighteen hours to be sure they were well away from the Comanches.

They would make it. Colt had no doubts. If he did everything exactly right, if he used all of his skills and understanding of the savages, he and the whole party would escape safely.

He couldn't sleep. Then a sudden exhaustion took hold of him and his head sagged and he slept. There were no dreams this time and just before eleven o'clock he woke.

He checked his watch. Hatchet had already sent his four best men to the horse pasture. They knew precisely what to do. There would be no stampede of the mounts until after some hue and cry from the camp made it certain that the captives had been discovered missing.

Colt tied everything down snugly on his mount. Made sure his headband was in place. Even during the movement through the camp he still had to look as much like an Indian as possible.

Colt, Hatchet and the last Tonk moved their horses toward the point agreed upon. Two of the Tonks would steal two good mounts early in the night and leave them at the appointed spot. Then the Indians would go back to the pasture area to be ready to kill the guards and turn loose the ponies and drive them over the ridge and down the next valley away from the White River Gorge.

Colt sat on the ground and waited. He had set twelve midnight as the best time to attack. That gave them six hours before daylight. It would be enough time. It had to be.

10

Major Colt Harding looked at his pocket watch in the faint moonlight. Midnight.

He lifted his hand to Hatchet. The two had tied their horses to small trees so a single yank of the end of the line would release the reins.

Both Hatchet and Colt took out their knives as they walked silently the twenty yards to the back of the big tipi. For the past hour they had not seen anyone move in the camp. They moved like slender shadows, never breaking a branch, not brushing a leaf filled branch, stepping carefully yet with purpose and authority.

They crouched a moment at the back of the tipi, then without a sound moved around to where the flap would be closed. They saw no one else near the other tipis as they paused at the flap. Hatchet lifted it and both men stepped in. It was almost dark inside, murkier than outside. A small flame still burned on an oak log in the fire. It blazed up and Hatchet pointed around to the left where the white woman slept with her arms on top of the buffalo robe.

Always Smiling, number one wife, lifted up from where she lay, awoke with a start and saw Hatchet three feet away even in the gloom. Hatchet's blade slashed through the air. Before the woman could make a sound the blade sliced her throat from side to side, opening both carotid arteries. She slumped back on her bed, her life gushing out the severed tubes in ten seconds.

Before she fell, Colt had slid noiselessly around the fire to where Sadie slept next to the outside of the big tipi. He shook her shoulder, then put his finger across her lips as she woke up.

He bent and whispered in her ear.

"I'm your daddy, Sadie, and I've come to take you home. Don't make a sound."

Hatchet had stopped at the white woman's bed, touched her shoulder, then put his hand over her mouth. Colt carried Sadie to the bed and whispered to the white woman.

"We're here to rescue you. Make no noise. Where is the boy?"

She nodded. Hatchet let go of her mouth. She felt under the buffalo robes and pulled up a sleeping bundle who mewed a moment at being moved, then slipped back to sleep.

The woman pulled on an Comanche dress of doeskin, stood quickly and picked up the boy. They moved quietly around the fire to the flap.

Near the back of the tipi, White Eagle snored softly, then rolled over and went on sleeping.

They stepped out of the tipi flap and hurried toward the woods. Not a word had been spoken aloud. The woman looked at Colt as they stopped at the horses. Earlier the second pair of horses had been brought.

"You're Sadie's father?" the white woman asked in a whisper.

Colt nodded. "Yes. Can you ride?"

She vaulted on the first pony's back and reached for the baby.

"I'll carry him," Colt said. Colt had lifted Sadie on one of the ponies, and then stepped up to his saddle and they moved upward over the hill and through the woods to the south. They had to go southwest to find the White River. They walked the horses until they were well away from the big Comanche camp.

Then they cantered for a while and Hatchet waved his arms and they galloped.

Colt was amazed at how well Sadie rode. She stayed glued to the pony's back like an Indian.

The woman rode alongside Colt when they slowed to a canter after ten minutes.

"My name is Doris Worthington," she said. "Mrs. Doris Worthington. That sweet little boy is Danny Ruger. He and I . . ." She paused. "He and I were captured at the same time. I've been looking out for him."

"Ma'am. I'm Major Colt Harding, Sadie's father. We better concentrate on riding. We can talk later."

Colt worked the party down the side of a small stream, then swung wide around a Comanche camp and slanted across the flatland toward where he figured the White River had to be. It was an easy way to find the gorge—just ride to the river and go downstream.

So far they had heard no outbursts behind them, no gunshots to alert the White Eagle band. They were more than a mile from the camp when they slowed again.

Colt rode near Sadie and watched her.

"Do you remember me?" he asked her.

Sadie looked over at Doris in the dim light. Doris nodded. Sadie smiled softly. "You are my daddy. I knew you would come and get me."

Colt blinked back tears and reached out and touched the small girl's shoulder, then her golden braids.

"I've found you, Sadie Harding, and nothing and no one will ever take you away from me again."

Sadie looked at the tall man who had Indian colored skin but a kind face. He wasn't really the way she remembered him at all. But she had been just a baby then. "I love you, Daddy," Sadie said.

Colt Harding couldn't control the tears that seeped down his cheeks. He picked up the pace. Where the hell was that damned river?

They rode for another half hour and then he saw the darker strip ahead. It had to be the White. It was larger than any of the others. They turned and rode down it, splashed across it in hock deep water and raced along quickly for a time, then slowed to give the horses a rest. Still nothing had been heard from behind them.

Just as he thought of it, Colt heard the faint sounds of gunfire back where the camp should be.

"They know you're gone, they'll be coming after us now. I just pray to God that the Tonks got rid of the horses in time."

Hatchet who had been leading the way dropped back. He nodded.

"Comanche Ponies all gone by now," he said. "They take fifty at time, drive north as soon as they get there."

"Just so the Comanches don't find them for three or four more hours."

Suddenly they were at the place where the White River plunged over a fifty foot falls down the side of the Cap Rock. They did not come up that way. They turned to the right and found the ravine two hundred yards down.

Hatchet stopped and looked at the descent.

"You remember coming up here?" Colt asked Doris and Sadie.

"It didn't seem this steep in the daylight," Doris said.

"Lead horses," Hatchet said. He got off his mount and he and the other Tonkawa went ahead, leading their sure-footed Indian ponies down the steep grade into the canyon that would bring them to the White River below the falls.

"I can lead my own pony," Sadie said. Colt motioned for her to go next. Doris went after her and Colt brought up the rear to act as rear guard. He still held Danny Ruger in one arm. Slowly he realized that little Danny wasn't Doris' child. That was a new element. He'd untangle that tomorrow—if they got away from White Eagle. He figured they had almost a two hour head start.

White Eagle had stirred once in his sleep, almost awoke, then drifted back to a heavy sleep. Then the dream came to him again, of Captain Two Guns raiding his camp and he sat bolt upright, scattering the buffalo robes. As he bent down to pick up one that had fallen near the fire he looked at Always

Smiling. She was his first wife and would always hold a special spot in his heart.

Now she lay half out of the robes. One arm was thrown out to the side and touched the floor of the tipi. That was unlike Always Smiling. She usually prided herself on how compactly she slept. Was she sick?

White Eagle lay there a moment listening to the others in the tipi breathing. Something was different. He jumped out of bed and in two strides looked at Always Smiling. He reached in to touch her arm. His hand came away sticky with drying blood.

The fire still danced giving off a dim light. He saw at once that Always Smiling was dead, her throat cut. He looked at his other wives, saw that they were safe, then went to the bed of the white slave.

She was gone.

The small boy was missing.

Laughing Golden Hair was gone as well.

White Eagle ran to the flap, grabbed his Spencer repeating rifle and blasted three shots into the air outside his tipi.

"Everyone up! There are killers in our Camp. Be alert! Look for the murderers."

The camp stirred. A dozen braves rushed out with their pistols.

From the horse pasture came shots and screams and the thunder of a thousand hoofs as they slammed into the ground.

"To the Ponies!" White Eagle screamed.

By the time thirty armed warriors raced to where the ponies had been kept three hundred yards from the last tipi, there were only half a dozen still in the big pasture. They had raced away, or been driven away, stampeding into the Staked Plains.

Five minutes later they found one of the herder boys. He had been killed with a knife. The other herder was missing.

"Captain Two Guns!" White Eagle muttered. He ran to find the first pony he could catch, threw a bridle on it and raced back to his tipi.

Every warrior he met he called the same orders.

"Round up a war pony, and send as many armed warriors as you can to the White River trail. Whoever raided us is heading down the trail with my white captives."

White Eagle stopped long enough at his tipi only to take his rifle and two boxes of rounds for it and his bow and a bundle of fifty arrows. Then he stormed through camp and rode as fast as the pony could go toward the White river trail.

He could hear other warriors behind him, but he was well out in front of them. How long for blood to dry? Always Smiling had been dead for an hour, maybe two. Not three. Whoever it was had stolen Doris and the boy and Laughing Golden Hair. That could only be Captain Two Guns.

White Eagle knew for certain that the Pony Soldier had not ridden onto the Staked Plains with a company of soldiers. He had come as an Indian, and struck as a Comanche, and turned for home. White Eagle felt a grudging admiration for the *tosi-tivo* warrior.

But such a great insult could not go unanswered. He would find the Pony Soldier and kill him slowly, then bring back the white captives.

People Eaters. Captain Two Guns must have brought the hated Tonkawa scouts with him as he had before. They had never been on the Staked

Plains. For a moment he felt defenseless. Not even here on the Staked Plains was the Comanche safe anymore.

He forgot it at once and rode harder. After nearly an hour of thunderous racing across the plains, the pony White Eagle rode on slowed and began to stumble. Quickly White Eagle stopped the mount and got down. The mare was blowing hard. She weaved for a moment, then went down on her front knees and rolled to her side. A moment later she was dead.

White Eagle fired his pistol in the air and a warrior rode up. It was Thunder Dog. He had found a stray pony on his ride and brought it along. White Eagle accepted the help gratefully and rode slower toward the White River.

An hour later White Eagle and Thunder Dog eased off their ponies at the ravine that led down to the White River trail. Thunder Dog got there first, and had taken his first step down the steep trail when a rifle spoke from below and a rifle slug slapped into the rocks near him and whined off into the prairie.

Thunder Dog leaped back from the lip of the trail out of sight of the gunman below.

White Eagle beat his fist against the pony three times, then dropped to the ground, edged up to the start of the trail and fired three rounds down the trail. There was no answering fire.

After five minutes, White Eagle crouched low and led his pony down the trail. The rifleman below did not fire.

White Eagle and Thunder Dog had to work down the trail slowly. There was no telling where the man with a rifle might be ahead. The racing, plunging, chattering waters covered up all but the loudest noises. A man could walk up behind you and you couldn't hear him coming.

White Eagle worked cautiously, yet still as fast as possible. He had not thought what he would do when he got to the bottom. What if there were a large force of Pony Soldiers there waiting for Captain Two Guns?

He and Thunder Dog would harass the soldiers and wait for the rest of the warriors to come. Surely fifty or sixty would find ponies and rush to help.

After what seemed like two hours, White Eagle and Thunder Dog reached the bottom of the White River Gorge. They slipped out quietly from the entrance and up to the bank.

There was not a shot, no response from anyone. Good.

Thunder Dog dismounted and put his ear to the ground. He stayed there too long. He changed positions. At last he stood and shook his head.

"I can hear nothing."

"We wait," White Eagle said. "With the sun we will track them down, and kill them all. These captives have been more trouble than I can put up with."

Colt and his party had worked down the White River Gorge carefully, trying not to rush. They were startled at the rifle shot behind them, but by that time they were nearly to the bottom and the shot came faintly over the sound of the water.

Hatchet lifted his hand and came up beside Colt.

"Shot, my men. Comanches have started down the gorge. My people catch up at the bottom if we wait for them."

Colt had agreed. He took Sadie and Doris and the baby a hundred yards downstream on the White and left Hatchet near the entrance to wait for his four men who had stampeded the Indian ponies.

Doris dismounted and walked over to Colt.

"If you had a shirt I could make a nest for Danny so I could tie him to my chest. Then you wouldn't have to carry him."

Colt reached in his small kit and took out his civilian shirt. Doris buttoned it up, slipped the neck hole over Danny's head and tied a knot in the tails, then one more snugging it up to his feet. She looped the sleeves of the shirt around her neck and cinched them up and asked Colt to tie them. She took off the rawhide belt she wore around her dress and tightened it around her back and the bulge that was Danny.

"All set," Doris said. "He can't fall off unless I do."

Sadie still sat on her pony. She shivered slightly in the cool night air. He reached in his kit and took out his clean shirt and put it on her. It was long enough to act as a dress.

"Are we really going to the fort?" Sadie asked softly.

Colt nodded and smiled. "We certainly are, Sadie. It will be your new home."

"And is Mommie there and Yale?"

Colt winced and looked away, glad that it was dark.

"No, Sadie. Your Mommie and Yale will not be there. I'll tell you about that when we are safe, away from the Comanche."

"They won't hurt us. They're my friends."

"White Eagle will not think so any more. He is my

enemy, because he stole you away from me. Now he will try to kill us all, so we must ride fast."

Colt had told Hatchet they could wait only fifteen minutes, then they would have to ride again.

Before that time Hatchet came up with his four mounted men, and they all rode forward.

Colt had worked out his escape plan on the way down the gorge. Now that they were on the plains, he would head due east. With any luck, White Eagle would have to wait for daylight to see what direction they went. Colt hoped that he would guess they went south toward Fort Comfort.

If so he might send half of his men that way. They could ride all night and be well out of the fight by morning. White Eagle might light torches and try to track them away from the White River.

Hatchet had been thinking the same thing. He sent his five men off in two's every mile or so to circle one side or the other and then return. He had the others ride spread out twenty yards apart so they wouldn't leave a concentrated trail.

Colt looked at the night sky. It was clear tonight and he could judge his direction. If he rode straight east he would be able to find Fort Brazos. It was about a hundred and twenty miles from the cap rock. Once he had circled around it on one of his clashes with White Eagle.

Now he hoped that he could find it. He figured he would have to move a little south of due east but not much. Half of his strategy counted on White Eagle picking the wrong destination.

Twice they stopped to rest the horses, let them drink and let the riders stretch their legs. Doris was holding up well. She was Comanche tough or she wouldn't have lasted in the Indian camp. Sadie was strong and resilient. To her it was still a lark, a change from what she usually did. She didn't really believe that her friend, White Eagle, would harm her or the others.

Colt took the headband off, washed the colored clay off his chest and face and arms. He let the crisp air dry him and shivered. But soon he was dry and felt better.

Hatchet had been putting his ear to the ground when they stopped. He shook his head. He could hear no horses behind them.

They had talked about putting two of Hatchet's scouts a mile or so behind them as a rear guard. At last they had decided against it. That might serve as a connecting link to give White Eagle a clue to their direction.

The break was over and they rode again. When it was about five o'clock by the fading stars, Colt called another stop. Colt figured they had made about twenty miles in the darkness. With any luck that would put them twenty miles ahead of White Eagle, if the Indian had waited or taken the bait and turned south.

Colt still had some of the beef jerky in his kit. He gave it to Doris and Sadie. Sadie sat by a small creek chewing the jerky and talking a steady stream to Doris. The woman had chewed up some of the jerky so it was soft and given it to Danny who was crying. She gave him water to drink from her hand, and he went back to sleep.

Sadie was talking about Black Bird and Something Pretty, White Eagle's two daughters who were both just a little older than she was.

"But I'm a better rider than they are. We used to borrow horses in the pasture when the herders weren't looking and practice riding until they caught us. That was fun. Will I get to ride horses at the fort?"

After a ten minute rest, Colt had them up and riding again. Hatchet had sent one of his men along their back trail to a slight rise and told him to wait there a half hour and watch for any pursuit, then to ride hard and catch up with them. He did. The Tonkawa could find no pursuit.

They rode steadily. Colt led them. An hour later they passed near the Croton Creek campsite where Colt had confronted White Eagle. They kept moving east.

If they had a hundred miles plus to ride, it would take them two full days of riding. They would have to stop and rest the horses in six to eight hours. They began hard riding about midnight. So by noon they had to find a hideaway where they could hole up and rest.

If White Eagle had provided each warrior with two mounts, there was a chance he could catch up with them as they rested. But if White Eagle had just one horse per warrior, he would have to be resting as well.

Colt thought it through again. If he had waited until he could track them at sunrise, he had to be thirty miles behind, maybe more. His swift little Indian ponies could cover that ground in four hours, if the trackers kept on the trail.

Spur turned to his lead scout.

"Hatchet, we ride until midday. How long can we rest and still stay ahead of White Eagle?"

"Maybe three hour. All Indian pony but one. Three hour plenty."

Colt pushed them hard. He led and had Hatchet

ride directly behind Doris. It was almost as if he were with the Lightning troop going to a fight. They cantered and galloped, then cantered and galloped. Every hour they stopped five minutes.

By ten o'clock they had covered another twenty-six or twenty-seven miles. They should be almost halfway to the fort, if they could find it.

During the past few miles they had gone over a few low hills, and now dropped down into a wide broad valley. Croton Creek flowed into the Brazos and Colt could see the river now on the left. It meandered around and swung north. Colt kept to his compass bearing of slightly south and east and they forged ahead.

Sadie looked tired. She was clinging to the Indian pony's mane now, but her knees gripped the mount firmly.

Doris had taken Danny off her chest and had him astride the horse in front of her.

Hatchet rode up, his face solemn.

"Comanches," he said and pointed slightly ahead of them and to the right.

Colt stared that way. Comanches was right. It looked like a whole band was on the move, strung out for a mile and headed directly across their line of travel.

11

"Keep moving, everyone!" Colt called. They had come together so they were riding in a group now, having abandoned the spread formation they used for a time.

Colt was evaluating the distance and the angle between his nine riders and the two hundred in the strung out Comanche band as it moved toward a new campsite. If he kept going at the current rate, his crew would pass in front of the long line of Comanches. He wondered if the Comanche warriors could spot a Tonk simply by looking at him.

"Hatchet. More of your enemies. Will they know you're Tonkawa just by watching you?"

"No. No should hurry."

"I agree. If we let them think we are afraid they could attack."

As he spoke a line of warriors with lances and

bows and shields rode out on the near side and around the front of the caravan.

"Just keep going, ignore them," Colt called. We wouldn't stand a chance in a fight, so we bluff it through. They must be on their way to their winter camp. They might not be in the mood for a confrontation either.

Colt saw three or four of the Indians conferring.

In fifteen minutes they would meet at the current pace. Colt let his horse stretch out just a little, to walk slightly faster. The others kept up. It was not a dramatic increase in speed, and the Indians couldn't have noticed it.

As the four Comanches left their conference, Colt thought he could tell that the Comanche march slowed just a little. If so they were going to let the small party of Indians pass in front of them with no confrontation.

Colt had not put on a shirt. He was one of them. They all could be mistaken for Indians at a distance. Especially since all but one of the horses were Indian ponies.

"Steady as it goes," Colt said. "Everybody hold tight and this will be over in about ten minutes. Hatchet, be sure your Tonks don't get some wild idea about having any Comanche soup from this band."

Hatchet spoke softly to the nearest Indian who passed the word to the other native Americans.

The two lines came closer together. The Comanches slowed even more and Colt increased the speed of his horse again. They would know in another two or three minutes.

Was it only a ruse to draw them in close so the warriors could surround and riddle them with arrows without a long chase? Or were these Comanches following the ages old custom that spring and summer were the times for war and raiding? Fall and winter were for hunting, making pemmican and working hard at trying to live through the cold times.

Colt looked straight ahead. He had picked out the point where their paths would cross. If they could break into a canter they would clear the other group easily. But he could not. It would seem like he was running away.

He pressed the big army mount a little faster. For a moment he looked out of the corner of his eye without turning his head. The Comanche line of marchers had come to a stop thirty yards from the trail Colt was on. They waited as the strangers passed by them.

There was no sign of recognition, no indication that either group saw the other. To do so would have required some type of communication, and that would have revealed the true identity of both sides and a fight would have been mandatory.

But this was fall, almost winter. It was not the time for war. So there would be no fight.

Colt cleared the other group by fifty yards, then he lifted his mount to a canter and the rest followed as they drove toward the east and a little to the south with the hopes of finding Fort Brazos.

When they were half a mile away, Colt turned and looked back at the Comanches. A group of six or eight warriors had ridden out a ways and stared at them, just checking, wondering what might have been. The woman and two children were heady prizes for such a small fight. The nine ponies were not to be forgotten either, but it was not to be.

They rode until one o'clock, found a stream that blushed with green trees, and slid off horses and stretched their aching bodies. Sadie yelped with delight and picked berries for all of them. She assured her father they were good. Then when she had her fill she sat down in the stream, squealing at the chill of the water, then coming out, shaking like a puppy, and sitting on the grass in the sun to dry.

Doris curled up on the grass and went to sleep.

Colt talked to Hatchet.

"How long can we rest the horses?"

"Three hours, no more. The Comanche band's tracks back there will confuse our tracks. Help."

"If only we knew how many warriors White Eagle gathered for the chase we would know better how to defend ourselves," Colt worried out loud.

As they talked more, they decided this was the time to send a rear guard. Hatchet would use his best man. He let his men rest for three hours, then one would stay there for an hour watching the back trail before he followed Colt and his band. If he saw the Comanches, he was to fly forward and let the main party know how many and how far behind they were.

Colt stood watch the first hour. Then Hatchet took over for the next two. At the end of the three hours everyone was back on his pony again and they all headed toward what they thought was a winding tributary of the Brazos River ahead of them another five miles. Colt remembered that the Brazos turned far to the north here in a wide loop.

Far behind Colt and his group, White Eagle was having problems with his warriors. Only twelve had found horses and had met below the gorge. He had hoped for many more. Even as the story spread of the murder of Always Smiling and the stealing of the white captives, few of the warriors thought it important enough to give chase.

Much time and work had been spent in rounding up the scattered horses. Some of the warriors were impressed by the way the horses had been driven away in several directions. Everyone in the camp knew that a warrior's horses were his wealth.

Most of the warriors felt it much more important to round up their own horses than to try to get back White Eagle's captives. If he wanted to run after them, that was his problem.

Some felt that the golden haired girl had been the cause of most of their troubles with the Pony Soldiers, and they were glad to see her gone. Now perhaps they could have some peace and not be harassed by the blue shirts.

White Eagle led his fourteen warriors out on the trail of Captain Two Guns once daylight came. They had circled the area three times before they found the fresh hootprints that moved east, not south as he figured. Where was the Pony Soldier Two Guns going?

They flew across the prairie, making good time. White Eagle knew that the Captain Two Guns's group would have ridden all night. They could be a day's hard ride ahead. But they would have to stop soon to rest their ponies.

From the hoofprints, White Eagle soon decided there were only nine ponies involved. One had been shod with the iron shoes, a cavalry mount.

So it was Captain Two Guns with his Tonkawa flesh eating devils. He must catch them.

By midday they had covered what White Eagle

figured were thirty five miles. By now the captives were still far ahead. Four of his warriors shook their heads and with no more explanation turned and rode back toward the Staked Plains. An hour later six more left and White Eagle came to a halt under a live oak tree near a stream and considered the matter. He only had four warriors with him.

Those four could leave at any time. He could not win a fight against two to one odds. But he could hurt the Captain Two Guns. He could hurt him badly. Hit fast and run, watch him, then strike again from ambush. Yes, he must do it. He called to his men and when the four of them rode up, he talked to them with great feeling and they understood.

"I have this fight. I must do it now so it will never bother our people again. We must hit this Captain Two Guns and drive him into the dirt. We must have him know that he can never again fight against the Comanche without understanding that we are the best warriors on the plains, and that we never give up, never run away or quit."

He looked at the men. Two were no more than sixteen years old, and held only their bows, not even a shield yet. Two were full warriors. They carried rifles.

"It will be a hard ride. They are far ahead of us, but we can ride like the wind, cut their trail and ride again. We can ride until our ponies nearly fall under us. We will catch them and use our long guns and send the bullets at them. Will you go with me?"

All four lifted their hands over their heads and shouted that they were with him.

They rode fast then, to the very point of breaking down their mounts. Then they rested a moment and drove forward again. The *tosi-tivo* and their

Tonkawa slaves were resting now. It was time to make up much lost ground.

Twice more they rode their ponies until the weakest began to show signs of stress. They slowed and walked, watered the mounts and then let all of them rest for a half hour. Then they were off riding again. The trail was plain now, the nine riders were grouped together with no attempt at evasion. They must feel that they had escaped. A gleam showed in White Eagle's eye as he pushed his four warriors faster.

He would kill Captain Two Guns first, then the white woman. The Tonkawas would run as soon as the captain was dead. Yes. It would work out well after all.

Less than three hours ahead of the Comanche hunters, Major Harding and his small group struggled forward. He could see that Doris was tiring. Sadie had nearly fallen off the horse once, and she insisted on having her ankles tied together under the mount.

"We do it all the time with the younger children," she said. "I'm tough enough to take it." She grinned. "I was a Comanche for a long time."

He tied her ankles together with a strip torn off the shirt she was wearing. It was still too big for her. He asked if that was too tight. She shook her head and reached up and kissed him, and Colt had to blink away tears.

Doris was another problem. She was tough and strong, but the idea of being rescued, at last, had set her to crying and she couldn't stop. She wept silently. Colt felt they should find someplace and hole up for a day and let everyone rest. But he knew that would be too dangerous with an unknown force of blood lusting Comanches behind them.

Now and then they saw the Tonkawa Indian scout who rode as their rear guard. He was a half mile to three miles behind them and kept in visual contact.

The country was open again, the small hills had been climbed and now there was just a long sweeping prairie that sloped gently toward where he figured the Brazos must be, to the far north and due east when it swung back south again. How many more miles was it to Fort Brazos and safety? Had this been a fool's mission that he could not win?

Colt had lost all track of the distances. They had been riding now for three hours since their rest. If they had averaged six miles an hour the first ten hours, that would be sixty miles. Since the rest they had come faster, maybe seven average, so they should be about eighty miles from the high rim rocks guarding the Staked Plains.

If White Eagle and his warriors had left at first light, they would have put in little more than eleven hours by now. If they had averaged six miles an hour, that would be sixty six miles. It was impossible for White Eagle to catch them before dark. Then he would have to wait again before he could follow the trail, unless he was a gambler.

He could either wait or make a wild guess and ride forward without any signs and hoping he was right.

Colt drew up beside Hatchet and asked him where he figured White Eagle might be by now. The short Indian stared at the dipping sun, then looked over his shoulder. He saw his scout a mile behind them.

"Comanches still two hours behind, even if they kill their ponies riding hard."

"And if we keep going during the darkness?"

"Then we go farther ahead," Hatchet looked

around. They were coming across a small creek that must lead into the Brazos. He smiled, then pointed.

"Hatchet and men stay here, wait for Comanche. When they come, we hunt for our soup. Major promised Comanche soup. This good time for soup."

Colt laughed softly. The Indian had a long memory. He looked over the dense brush and trees. It was an ideal ambush spot. If Hatchet had decided to do it, there was nothing he could do to prevent it. Such a stroke could decimate any chase group of Comanche, and might send them running, bloody and wounded, back toward the Staked Plains.

Colt nodded. "Hatchet, you do what you want. We'll be heading dead east from here. See that small notch up there where the sun is almost hitting? We'll be using that landmark. You find us before noon tomorrow. Understand?"

Hatchet grinned, nodded and said something to his men and they wheeled away from the others into the woods.

Doris came up quickly. "What in the world?"

"Rear guard," Colt said quickly. "Hatchet and his men will stay here and ambush the Comanches if there are any back there tracking us. If he can stop them here, we have clear sailing into Fort Brazos. We'll ride out and keep moving at a walk until midnight. That way we should be twenty-five miles closer to the fort."

"So we'll get there tomorrow?" Doris asked. She put one hand to her head and brushed back the dark hair that she had undone from the braids. It danced around her face in curls from being braided for so long.

"I'd hope so. Maybe twenty miles tomorrow." His voice changed, lowered, softened. "How are you holding up?"

"I'd love to get six or eight hours of sleep." She grinned. "But this is just lots better than the past two months with the Comanches." She had stopped crying at last. "I'm sorry about all the tears. I got started thinking about home—where I used to live with my family—and it just came. I'm better now. Another six hours? No problem for me."

The three horses moved ahead, Colt in the lead picking the trail, Sadie in the middle and Doris and little Danny at the back. There was no more talk of Indians. They rode through the pure, wild, untarnished Western Texas prairie. It seemed never to end to the east ahead of them. But it would soon end in darkness which would sweep down on them all too soon.

Colt kept moving ahead, wondering what would happen behind them. There might be no Comanches following. Hatchet didn't know for sure. He was thinking as an Indian would, so he was probably right. If the Comanche force was too large to confront, Colt knew that Hatchet would simply let the group pass, fade away and ride around them and back to his employer.

Colt wished that he could be there and see what took place. Instead he angled along a small stream, across it and kept on his eastward angle.

Hatchet looked over the area critically. He figured where the Comanches would come in and spotted his men at precise positions so they would have a crossfire without endangering each other. His rear guard Tonkawa scout rode in and they all jumped out and screamed, scaring him into bolting forward. He came back when he saw who had yelled. They screamed at him and teased him for being caught off guard.

He was added to the ambush. The rear guard told Hatchet that he had not seen anyone following them. If the Comanche were coming they were still several miles back.

Hatchet watched the sun sink lower. There was still time. The Comanches would be pushing as hard as they could. Even if they came just after dark, there would be a big moon tonight and no clouds to spoil the light.

They waited.

Colt had made sure that all of his scouts had Spencer repeating rifles for this trip. Now they polished the weapons as they waited. Colt had personally instructed each of the Tonkawas how to sight and fire the weapons. Three of the men were good natural shots. The other two were passable. Hatchet was probably the second best shot at the fort.

The sun sank lower.

A half hour later the tinges of dusk filtered through the trees.

Then the most outward scout made a signal. He had seen someone coming.

Two minutes later a ragged group of Comanches cantered toward the river brush. White Eagle was leading them, watching the ground. He paused and said something to the men, then they came on. They were almost in the trap.

Hatchet had berated his men that if they shot before all the Comanches were in the right spot, they would get no soup. Their eyes lit up and he knew they would wait.

He told them not to fire at White Eagle. He would

be the tallest man, the leader. He must get away. Even though he was an enemy, the Comanche was too good an Indian to kill this way.

Hatchet was surprised when he saw only four warriors with White Eagle. He had not bothered to assign definite targets. He doubted if the Tonks would have listened to that anyway. They would fire at anyone who was alive, except the chief.

"*Ho-ha!*" Hatchet bellowed and six rifles blasted into the stillness of the Texas wilderness. Two Comanches fell from their ponies dead as they hit the ground. Two others dug feet into ribs but a second ragged volley shot them off their ponies as well. Only White Eagle survived.

He had charged his horse forward into the woods, almost run down one of the Tonks who dove to one side. White Eagle had no time to use his rifle. Then he went charging through the brush, getting as far away from the ambush as possible.

He had seen two of his men go down. He was sure the other two had been shot down as well. Now all he could hope for was to outdistance the attackers. They must be the Tonkawa, the hated People Eaters.

Far behind him he heard a Tonkawa war cry and he bit his lip until his teeth drew blood as he raced away. It was a double day of shame for him. He was not certain he was worthy to have a band of his own. He would confer with the great spirits tonight. Tomorrow he would make his sad way home to the Staked Plains and try to get the move started into the winter camp.

At the site of the ambush, Hatchet yelled at his men to catch the ponies. They could use them as spare mounts. Quickly the four horses were caught and tied to bushes. Then the Tonkawas stared at their victims. They would take the scalps, and carry them until they met with the Pony Soldiers, then quickly discard them because it was against Pony Soldier rules to take scalps.

But there was other work to do, far more important, and far more delicious.

One of the men cleared a space and brought rocks and made a fire near the creek bank. Others took out their sharpest knives and moved toward the bodies of the Comanche warriors where they lay sprawled in death in the near darkness.

Hatchet settled back on the grass. It had been his plan, his men would feed him. He was more firmly their chief now than ever before. His mouth watered as he thought of the delicacies that would be brought to him. They would more than eat their fill tonight.

Tomorrow they would eat again, then using the spare ponies to trade off riding, they would rush ahead and catch up with Major Harding.

Hatchet wondered what he would do with the new ten dollar gold piece he was earning? He would go to the Sutler's store and walk up and down the aisles trying to decide. It would be a glorious day for him. One that he would never forget. All of this and soup too. He could combine the best of Tonkawa skills and traditions, and the wealth and goods of the Pony Soldiers.

12

Colt Harding and his three charges were more than an hour and a half away from the ambush spot when darkness closed around them. The major had been listening to the rear, but had heard no rifle fire. He didn't know if that was good or bad.

It either meant they were too far away to hear the shots, or that no shots had been made by Hatchet. No shots could mean a large force of twenty or thirty Comanche warriors had ridden in and Hatchet stayed in place, then left quietly when the Comanches had passed.

Damnit! He wanted to know which one happened.

Colt tried to put it out of his mind. They were moving along a small stream again, then crossed it and swung a little farther south to follow a gentle valley between low ridges. Not really mountain ridges, more like humps in the plains. The country had flattened out again with little to keep them from riding a direct line east.

Colt struck a match and checked the time. Seven-thirty P.M. They had a long ride before they could stop. Even then would they be safe from the Comanche?

By that time there would be little choice. Twice Sadie had almost fallen off her horse. She had caught the mane at the last moment before she would have slipped down with her torso hanging from the shirt strip that held her ankles tied together.

Doris was holding up well now. It seemed that the harder the ride became, the stronger she grew. She joked and talked with Sadie to keep her awake. Danny had cried again and they found him some berries he liked, then she gave him some more of the jerky that she had saved. This time she let him soak it up in his mouth and work on it with his baby teeth. It kept him quiet for an hour.

Danny sat astride the Indian pony in front of Doris and she held him in place with one hand.

Colt looked at them with admiration. They could teach his Lightning Company a thing or two about determination, that was sure.

Another hour dragged by, then two. There was no sound at all now, not of shots or water nor animals. Now and then a night bird screeched, or an owl hooted. But usually the silence lay so thick around them that they could almost pour it.

By eleven-thirty, Colt said "enough" and called a halt. He found a small feeder stream with thick brush. They tied the horses close by in case the Comanche came and he left the saddle on the army mount. He couldn't risk taking it off.

Colt assured Doris it was safe.

"The Comanche could have been turned back by Hatchet and his men, if they followed us this far at all. Chances are Hatchet encountered no one but our own rear guard and they all will find us in the morning. Then we'll know for sure what happened back there."

"Shouldn't one of us stay awake?" Doris asked.

"No. There's no chance that the Comanches could make up the head start we have on them. Especially not since we just put six hours more distance away from them. They can't track us during the night."

"But . . ."

He touched her shoulder and could see in the soft moonlight that she was half asleep already. She had bedded down little Danny and Sadie next to each other, with the two shirts covering both of them.

"Settle down beside them. I'll let you know if anything happens. Hey," he said gently. "This is the Army and I'm your commanding officer, so settle down and get some sleep. I'll see you in the morning."

She sighed, lay down beside the children and was sleeping before he turned away.

Colt knew he was right about the Comanche. Still he walked around the camp. It felt good to walk again after so many hours of riding. He could use the sleep, but he didn't relish letting White Eagle find them all snoring. He would watch and listen for a while.

An hour later he sat by a sturdy pecan tree and looked to the west. He wouldn't go to sleep, just rest a little bit. Just rest, maybe close his eyes for a moment.

Something warm touched his face.

Colt pawed at it to brush it away, but it was still there. He scratched at it and then suddenly he was wide awake. The critter on his face was a beam of sunshine boring through some holes in the branches and leaves above him. A quick look at his watch showed that it was almost eight o'clock.

The next thing he saw was Doris who sat across from him, a smile on her face.

"You looked so peaceful I couldn't bear to wake you. How long did you stay on guard duty last night?"

"Not long." He shook his head. "We better be moving. You can bet your last pony that White Eagle is riding hard."

The children were both up. Sadie ran up with a double handful of berries she had picked. More lay on a large leaf near Doris.

"Breakfast? They're good, whatever they are."

Sadie picked up something else.

"Look, wild onions. Always Smiling taught me how to find them. There's a lot of things around here we can eat."

She had washed the onions in a tiny trickle of a spring near by. Colt popped one of them into his mouth and chewed. It was mild, but they were still onions. Enough to keep one from starving. He had a handful of the berries, then when they were gone the small caravan mounted up.

"Today we get to Fort Brazos," Colt said. He looked at Doris. "Hear anything like six Tonkawa Indians coming up?"

"Not a thing."

They rode.

The country flattened out even more. It was a grassland, pure and pristine. Waving miles of foot high grass that was now brown and had fallen down and matted in some places. Come spring and the ground would send bright new shoots through the matt and soon there would be miles and miles of green again.

Colt found the notch in the far off ridge he had been following when he could see it, and they rode faster. He alternated cantering and galloping, to speed the miles away.

They saw no one. There was still no sign of any settlers, but miles and miles of grasslands that could be used for ranching and probably farming near the rivers.

At ten o'clock they came to a slight rise and Colt stopped on the top to look east.

He caught his breath. Less than five miles away he saw a column of smoke rising in the air. To the north he could see the large green snake of a river and its brushy and tree-filled banks. They were close to something.

"The smoke," Doris said. "Is that the fort?"

"I hope to God it is and not some settler burned out by some rampaging Comanches."

They hurried down off the rise, but there was little they could do to conceal themselves and still move toward the smoke. At last they broke into the open from a small stream they had been following.

"Let's see what it is," Colt said. "There can't be any Comanches this far to the east."

They rode another hour and then came through a screen of trees. Axes rang against wood as a dozen blue shirted troopers worked on a wood detail.

"We made it!" Colt said.

Doris began to cry with joy.

Sadie looked at both of them in surprise then

nudged her horse forward. "I want to see the fort," she said, all practical and businesslike.

They rode up to the wood detail. Colt talked to a sergeant in charge who told one of his men to lead them to the fort.

"Major, you've had a long ride. We've heard of Fort Comfort. Isn't that where that Lightning Company is billeted?"

"That's the place, Sergeant. Now we better get moving. Oh, are there any women at your post?"

"Yes sir, officers' wives mostly. More than a dozen, I'd reckon."

"Thanks, Sergeant."

Twenty minutes later they rode through the gate and inside the adobe block walls of Fort Brazos. It was about the same size as Fort Comfort. Colt turned toward the west side, but the private indicated the commander's office was on the other side in officer country.

Colt stepped down stiffly from his army saddle and then helped Doris down and little Danny. Sadie had slid down expertly by herself.

"It's big, isn't it?" she said looking around. "Are all of these men really Pony Soldiers?"

Colt picked her up and carried her as they followed the soldier up the small steps to the door that he held open.

Inside, it looked almost like his own office. A sergeant sat behind a small desk. An adjutant shared the room and an open door led to the second office.

The private spoke to the sergeant who nodded at Colt and hurried into the other office.

A short, red haired captain bustled out. He started to salute then stopped.

"Maj . . ." he bit off the word halfway through.

Colt dug into his back pocket and took out his orders, promoting him to major, and handed them to the captain.

"Well, yes. Major Harding. I've heard about you. Lightning Company and all that. Come in. Madame, and children, come in, please."

It took a half hour for Colt to get the matter settled. What he wanted was simple. Clothes for Sadie and Doris and the small boy. Then he wanted an escort south to Fort Comfort.

"Major, you don't ask much."

"Captain. This small girl is my daughter. She was captured by the Comanche nearly six months ago when her mother and brother were killed in a raid on a supply train. This lady is Doris Worthington, who saw her whole family killed in a Comanche raid west of here. She was kept by the band's chief, White Eagle.

"Oh, yes, I'll have six Tonkawa scouts coming to the fort soon. I'd like them given permission to camp nearby until we leave for Fort Comfort."

"You . . . ah . . ." the captain looked at him and then at the three civilians. "You and six Tonks rescued these three captives from White Eagle. All by yourselves?"

"Yes, Captain. I tried it twice with a company of cavalry. It didn't work. This way did work. I used Indian tactics on the Indians. Hell, I even looked and smelled like an Indian. But it worked. Now can you help me get this lady and these two children down to Fort Comfort or not?"

The captain grinned and nodded. "Yeah, the Lightning Company. That's yours, right? Heard about it. True that you can take a company of cavalry over seventy five miles in a day?"

"Yes, and be ready to fight. It's all in my report. We'd like to rest today, and move out first thing in the morning, Captain. I'd think that twenty troopers would be sufficient. Call it a training march."

"Of course, yes. Never any doubt. Sergeant Foster!" His voice rose. The sergeant hurred in the door. He scrawled a note on a pad of paper and gave it to the sergeant. "Take that over to my wife and escort her back here just as soon as possible."

"Yes, sir."

For the next fifteen minutes the captain questioned Colt about his Lightning Company, how it worked, who could apply, how they selected the men. Then when Colt was getting a little bit unhappy about the whole thing, a door opened and a woman just about Doris's size came into the room.

"Olden, you might have told me we were having company. Now you men get out of here, Doris and I have some work to do." She knelt in front of Sadie. "And this must be Sadie. How are you, pretty little girl?"

Sadie stared at the woman's beautiful dress and reached out and touched it.

"Pretty," she said.

When the men were shooed out of the room, the woman turned to Doris.

"My name is Mary Longstreet. Captain Longstreet is my husband and we have two boys and two girls. What we're going to do is give you something a little more standard to wear."

She looked at Doris, then moved to her and hugged her tightly. She blinked back tears.

"Doris, I know you've had a terrible time, and what I'm going to say might hurt just a little, but we need to do it and get it over with. You look sturdy to me."

They both smiled.

"Most of the 'proper' army wives and civilians too, don't think kindly of a woman who has been captured by the Indians and then rescued. They know that she's been used by the Indians, and they think this taints her some way. Lord knows, and you and I know, that an Indian man isn't that much different from a German or an Irishman or an Englishman.

"You know what I'm saying, Doris?"

"Yes," she said softly. "I'd . . . I'd heard stories like that when we were in the frontier."

"So, we're going to outfit you with clothes. Then you and the children will stay in the visiting dignitary quarters tonight, and nobody will know any different than that you came in from Wichita Falls or someplace."

She looked at Doris critically, tightened the Indian dress around her bosom.

"Yes, it should fit. You're bigger on top than I am but I can let it out a little if need be. I'm handy with a needle and thread. Now, slip out of that Indian dress and I'll trade you for this calico, even up."

Doris began to cry. Mary put her arms around her and patted her shoulders.

"There, there. When we get you and the kids over to our quarters, I'll fix you up with a bath and some underthings, and a valise I don't need any more. We'll have you all fit and proper in side of two hours. Now, take off that Indian dress."

When the ladies came out of the captain's office a half hour later, Doris' long hair had been combed until it shone. Her face was washed clean and so were her hands and arms. She wore the calico dress with dignity and charm. There were button shoes on her feet.

Sadie now wore a child's dress that she said was too tight. She had on shoes, too, and looked like a little lady.

Mary Longstreet smiled at Colt. "Sergeant Foster is bringing you a proper uniform from the quartermaster, Major Harding. Mrs. Worthington and I have some things to do. We'll see you for supper at my quarters. Tell Olden that about six o'clock will be fine."

She and Doris and the children went out the door. Doris gave Colt one fleeting glance. She was smiling.

Major Harding gave Captain Longstreet a complete rundown on his Lightning Company. "What it boils down to, Longstreet, is that you must have one officer who will bust his ass to select and train the men. It can't be done from the officer's quarters.

"The commander of that company must be able to shoot under his horse's neck, or his men won't learn how. He has to be the best rider in the company, the best shot, able to ride a hundred miles in twenty-four hours without stopping if he has two horses. It is simply one hell of a lot of work.

"Then on top of that you have to find forty men who are willing to do the extra work at no extra pay."

Captain Longstreet sat back down at his desk. "At least I know how to do it now if I ever really want to. Now, Foster has your new uniform. I'll trade it to you even up for the information about your Lightning Company.

"Foster will take you to one of the vacant officers

quarters where you can take a bath and have a rest and then get dressed for dinner. Six o'clock I hear."

Foster came in and talked to the captain quietly for a moment.

"Yes, thanks, Sergeant. Foster tells me that your Tonks have arrived. They have been positioned outside the fort at the creek a quarter of a mile off. They have been told to be ready to ride first thing in the morning.

"Oh, my sergeant says the Tonkawa scouts seem to be in an unusually happy mood. What happened?"

"You really don't want to hear about all of the grisly details, Captain, if I'm right. Now where is that bath water?"

An orderly made a fire for Colt in the stove in his temporary quarters, filled two boilers with water to heat and then brought in a midday lunch for him of two big sandwiches, a pot of black coffee steaming hot, and two apples. Captain Longstreet had sent along a pint of bourbon whiskey.

Colt lay down on the bed and nearly let the fire go out. He stoked the stove again with split wood and when the water was hot, poured it in a portable bathtub about the size his mother used to wash clothes in. It was cramped but practical.

After his bath he dressed in the new underwear and field uniform with its yellow stripe up the blue pants leg and blue shirt. It even had his major's rank sewn on the shoulders. Then he lay down on the soft bed and went to sleep.

Captain Longstreet came inside to wake him up just before six o'clock.

The dinner was a smashing success. Colt stared at Doris when he first came into the captain's quarters. Her hair had been washed and combed until it was a black froth around her face. Her skin had been scrubbed and some lotion put on it until it glowed.

Then there was the dress, which showed a lot of Doris that he hadn't noticed before in her squaw dress. He stared until Doris giggled, then he looked at Sadie. Her hair had been washed as well and combed. It flowed around her like a golden halo and waterfall.

"Do you like my new dress, Daddy?" Sadie asked. He swept her up and gave her a big kiss, then carried her to the dinner table.

Even Danny had on a little pair of pants and a shirt. One of the women on the post had a child about Danny's age and she supplied two sets of clothes for him.

Colt was flabbergasted.

"I really don't know what to say. How can I ever repay you? These ladies have been through a lot in the last few months."

"I just want to make sure their suffering is over," Mary Longstreet said. "You know how folks talk about a woman captive who is rescued. They won't talk that way about Doris. We won't give them the chance. We've got it all worked out.

"It's about the same distance from here to Austin as it is to Fort Comfort. What we're going to do is return you to Austin instead of . . ." She looked up sharply as Colt lifted his hand to interrupt.

"Hear me out, Major," she said sharply.

Captain Longstreet coughed. She sent him an angry glance and went on.

"Women are hard to fool, Major. You come into the Fort with Doris and Sadie, what are they going to think? They'll know for sure that you rescued all three of them. So we won't let that happen.

"Doris will stay in Austin with my sister until the next supply wagon goes out to Fort Comfort. She'll arrive with her small son to visit her brother-in-law, the camp commander. She's a recent widow from Cleveland. Doris is a relative of sorts, but not a blood relative, and she has no one else."

Doris looked at Colt whose frown had changed to a smile.

"Yes, yes. That will work out well. I do want you to come to the fort. It's not a hardship post."

Doris nodded and looked away.

"Now that we have that settled, let's have something to eat." The food was delicious and Colt ate more than he should. They talked and visited for a while, then Colt reminded them they had an early morning ride.

Colt walked Doris and Sadie back to their quarters. He carried little Danny who had gone to sleep on a rug near the fireplace.

"I'm glad you agree that I should stop in Austin. I hadn't thought any farther than this place."

"We can thank Mary Longstreet for that," Colt said. "And I do want you to come to the fort. I . . . I want to get to know you better. We have to figure out what to do with little Danny. There are still a lot of questions."

At the door of the visitors' quarters he paused. She watched him for a moment.

"Colt, I hear in China when you save someone's life, that person is your slave for life. I . . . you know you saved my life. I wish this were China." She turned and hurried into the quarters with Sadie and closed the door. Then she opened it and pushed Sadie out.

"Kiss your father goodnight, Sadie," Doris said.

Colt swept Sadie up in a big hug and kissed her cheek. He put her down and she scurried inside.

He walked slowly back to his quarters. He knew damn well what Doris Worthington had meant. He just didn't know if he was ready to accept the idea yet.

13

The trip to Austin started on schedule. Relieved of his guarding duties, Colt took over Danny and carried him on his mount. Mary Longstreet had found an old Army pack and cut holes in it for Danny's legs and fixed the straps so Colt could wear it on his chest giving Danny a lot of freedom of movement but still be solidly held in place.

They rode out with twenty troopers and Lieutenant Quigley in charge. They figured the trip would last four days, and sent along a Sibley conical tent for Doris and Sadie. It was loaded on a pack mule along with a small stove and two folding chairs. Another pack carried extra rations for the civilians.

The first night Colt figured they had covered about forty miles at the leisurely pace. It felt natural to him, but slow. Mrs. Longstreet had found a split skirt made of soft doeskin which she gave Doris for the ride.

As they left the fort that morning, Doris had thrown her arms around Mrs. Longstreet and hugged her. Tears of joy seeped from her eyes.

"You're the most wonderful, unselfish person I've ever met, Mary. I just hope your husband and all the rest of the people here at Fort Brazos appreciate you." Then she whispered. "I don't want to embarrass you, Mary. But from now on, I'm going to try to be as wonderful to people as you are."

When the tent was put up that first night Colt went over to approve. Doris asked him inside to inspect it. He knew the Sibley well. It was standard issue for officers on a long hike. The troops used shelter halves that made into "pup" tents. There was even a small lantern.

"Isn't this a nice tent, Daddy?" Sadie asked.

"It sure it, and you get to sleep in here for three or four nights."

Sadie soon went to bed, tired out after the extended trip. Doris looked at Colt as they sat in the chairs. The heat from the small lantern had warmed the inside of the tent comfortably.

"Colt Harding, I want to tell you about what happened to me before you met me."

Colt held up his hand. "Doris, it isn't necessary. I know a lot about you since I met you."

"That's not enough. I want you to know everything. I was married when I was seventeen to George Worthington. He was a farmer. Five families of us went from East Texas to a place just fifty miles west of Fort Worth. The officers at the fort said they couldn't protect us out fifty miles, but we figured with five families we would be safe.

"We weren't. One day the Comanches came. Before I could even move, my two year old son was dead. A Comanche picked him up by his feet and swung him around and . . . " She looked away. "I saw George go down with three arrows in his chest. Then someone hit me from behind and I fell to the ground. When it was over, White Eagle put me on a horse. He had found Danny, and I cared for him. We were the only ones left alive."

"That's all over now," Colt said sharply. "We're going to Fort Comfort. You can start a new life. You can do anything you want to."

"No I can't. I'm a widow. I never went past the sixth grade. I'm a farm girl." She looked up, bit her lip and went on. "And what's more important, the Comanches, that is White Eagle, used me. He made love to me, in bed. I want you to be sure to understand that. I couldn't fight him, I never did. It wasn't any different than with my husband. Does that . . . does that make me a fallen woman? Does that make me dirty and unclean?"

Colt stared at her. Did it? Should she have fought and died instead of submitting? He shook his head.

"Doris, you're a wonderful person, a fine woman. You're a widow. You are not dirty or unclean. I think you're marvelous the way you've stood up under conditions that would send a Pony Soldier on a drunken binge."

She reached out and touched his shoulder. Just to be touching him. "Thank you, Colt. I'm so grateful that you understand. I don't care what anyone else thinks, except you and Sarah. You've both become very important to me."

Danny cried in his sleep and she moved at once,

putting a blanket back over him, rubbing his forehead until he relaxed again in a deep sleep.

"Doris, what other people think is important if you have to live in that community. Let's play out this plan, and when you get to the fort, we'll see what we can work out. Sadie has become very attached to you."

"Thank you, Colt. Now, I want you to tell me about your wife, and your son. Please. I know it's hard, but I really want to know what happened. I can see that you loved her very much."

He told her about the Indian raid on a cavalry supply train coming from Austin to Fort Comfort. Usually the Comanches did not come in that far, but this time they did and overwhelmed it.

"It was White Eagle, and he took Sadie as a captive, and they killed everyone else."

"I'm so sorry, and I do know a little of how it feels to have lost loved ones."

They talked a few minutes more, then he said goodbye and went to his blankets. They had agreed to start an hour later in the morning than the usual six o'clock trail time.

Six days later they came into Austin. They found Mrs. Longstreet's sister's house and gave her a letter the captain's wife had written. Harriet Johnson was a lot like her sister, short and slender and always in motion. She took Doris over like a lost child, cuddled Danny and said she would take care of them for a week, then contact the cavalry camp about the first wagon going to Fort Comfort. One should be leaving in a week or so.

Colt had left his Tonkawas outside the small town. He said goodbye to Doris and Danny, released the twenty men under Lieutenant Quigley and set out with a small pack of food for the trail to Fort Comfort. It was only a little over a hundred and twenty miles. He and Sadie and his Tonks would make it in two days.

He bought two sturdy blankets and tied them over the Army mount with a girth strap to give Sadie a softer seat on the horse. She said she didn't want a saddle after trying one at Fort Brazos.

When they were only two miles away from Fort Comfort, Colt saw a patrol come out to investigate them. There were six troopers and one was Sergeant Casemore. He rode up and skidded to a halt, popped a stiff, perfect salute that could not hide the grin on his big open face.

"Sergeant Casemore welcomes the Major back to his post, sir. It's good to have you home." He turned to the young girl. "And this must be Sadie. I bothered Captain Riddle until he told me what you were really up to."

"Sadie, meet Sergeant Casemore. One of the best soldiers in the cavalry."

She looked up and nodded, then looked away.

Half the camp was on the parade grounds when Major Harding and his little band rode in. Hatchet and his scouts angled off for their village on the creek.

It took Sadie two days to settle down and realize this was where she was going to stay.

"We get these rooms, all to ourselves?" she asked Colt.

"I'm the Fort Commander," he told her. "I'm the leader of this band of soldiers."

"Mommie isn't here, is she?"

"No, she and Yale . . ."

"I heard you and Doris talking in the tent. I really

wasn't sleeping. She's dead. And White Eagle's warriors did kill her. I didn't know for sure. He threw her out of the wagon and then Yale ran toward him with a knife he had . . . but he ran onto White Eagle's knife. I thought it just hurt Yale, but . . . but it killed him."

She cried then, and Colt held her closely.

"They're gone, Sadie. That leaves just you and me. But I'm going to take care of you, and protect you. And you'll never have to worry about winter snow, or having enough to eat or how to stay warm. Maybe, someday, we'll find a new lady to live at our house, would you like that?"

"Doris?" Sadie asked suddenly.

"Maybe, you never can tell about grown-ups. They get funny ideas sometimes. Just be patient with us. All right?"

"All right, Daddy. Now, you said you'd tell me a story about when you were a little boy back East somewhere."

He told her two stories, then she went to bed in her own room and dropped off to sleep.

The next day Colt got back to running his fort.

Captain Riddle stared at him a minute, then shook his head. "You'll have to tell me about it some night over a glass of good whiskey, Colt. I really never thought you'd come back from that trip. I figured you as Comanche meat out there somewhere. Seven just don't go up against a hundred Comanche braves and come out winning very often."

Colt laughed. "We pulled a dirty trick on them. We played like we were Comanche and did it the way they would have. They are damned good fighting men."

"There are a few papers on your desk."

"I noticed. Anything from Colonel Sparkman?"

"Three or four. He's busting a bridle to come out here for a visit. But he wanted to be sure you were here."

"That mean I'm in trouble?"

"Doubt it. He wants of review of your Lightning Company."

Colt nodded. "Good. Have Sergeant Swenson get Lieutenant Petroff in here. I want to know how his troops are doing. How are the other new officers working out?"

"Fine. All except Lieutenant Schultz. We sent him on a wagon heading to San Antonio with a guard three days ago."

"Had to be done. Send Petroff in as soon as he gets here."

Three days later a courier arrived with a single wagon from Austin and a twelve man escort. Unusual. In the wagon rode Mrs. Doris Worthinggon and a small boy, Danny.

Colt met them as soon as he heard they had come in the gate. He gave his sister-in-law a peck on the cheek and took her and Danny into his private quarters.

Sadie screeched in delight when she saw Doris. They hugged and danced around. Then Sadie began playing with Danny.

Doris turned to Colt, her eyes dancing. "Mary Longstreet's sister is a most forceful woman. She went to see the captain at the cavalry post in Austin the second day I was there and rattled the whole place. She was wonderful. Her husband is a banker in Austin."

"I'm glad you're here. I've missed you. Sadie has talked of nothing else since we left you."

"Good. Officially, I'm your sister-in-law here on a visit. Is that still all right?"

"Of course. We'll get you situated in an empty officer's quarters for now."

"And later, Colt? What about later?"

"We'll have to wait and see. One thing you'll learn about the Army. She is a most demanding mistress, and calls the shots. The Army screams and I jump. The Army comes first."

"Yes, I can tell. Where are we to stay? I'm anxious to get unpacked and see the new things I bought."

He looked up. "Bought?"

"Yes. I found two gold eagles in an envelope left for me with Mrs. Johnson. Would you know anything about that?"

Colt grinned. "Haven't the slightest idea. But it's a good thing you got some clothes. How would it look for my sister-in-law to show up on a visit with only one dress."

"Strange. Now, can I come over here and fix dinner for you and take care of Sadie while you're working?"

"I'm never far away from her, but . . . why not."

"Danny and I will go back to our quarters every night."

"Sounds like a good arrangement for me."

Doris smiled and touched his arm. "And a good situation for me and Danny. I've decided to keep him. I knew Danny's parents. I can't stand to see him go to somebody else to raise. So, I've got a son back again."

"Congratulations."

He took them to the new quarters. He'd had it heated and stocked with enough food and provisions for a month before she arrived. There were blankets and sheets, and towels and all the items Doris might need. There was no crib but there were two bedrooms.

Doris looked around and sat down on a chair suddenly because her legs wouldn't hold her up. She fought back tears and Sadie came over and hugged her.

"That help?" Sadie asked.

Doris burst out laughing and hugged Sadie back, then wiped away the moisture and stood.

"Thank you very much, Major, for all your kindness. I'd like to invite you to dinner here at my quarters tonight, about six. Can Sadie stay with us until then?"

Colt nodded and hurried out the door before he said something that he didn't think he was quite ready to say. It ground around in him until he was back behind his desk, looking over daily reports, checking on quartermaster orders and getting back in to the flow of his job.

Captain Riddle came in. "That's an extremely nice sister-in-law you have. You never told me that you lost a brother."

"Oversight. Sorry. How is that new quartermaster working out for you."

"Fine. He needs a little training, but I can do that an hour a day instead of spending half my time over there. Thanks."

"Sergeant Swenson!" Colt called.

Swenson was there in a moment. "Yes, sir, Major?"

"Tell Petroff there'll be an all day training session for the Lightning Company tomorrow. Have the men bring rations for one meal to cook. We'll be back late. Oh, also tell him to bring along the top five men waiting to get into the company."

"Yes, sir." Swenson left.

"John, I'd bet a month's pay that Colonel Sparkman will be paying us a visit within the next week or two. You'd better use some men and get this post spruced up. Do everything we've been putting off. And put a double crew to work on the adobe. I want all the waiting adobe blocks mortared in place before Phil gets here."

"We'll try. We have about two hundred out there waiting."

"Good, pull out all the masons and get them working. I have to get Lightning Company razor sharp for what I figure is going to be an inspection to end all inspections, and then some field testing." Colt snorted. "I just hope Phil plans to come along. We'll ride his tail right into the dirt."

Dinner that night at Doris's quarters was simple: roast beef, peas, carrots and potatoes, and apple pie.

Colt sat back and put down his napkin. "Good thing I don't eat this way every day or I'd grow so fat I couldn't get on my horse."

"Isn't Doris a good cook, Daddy?" Sadie said a big broad smile on her face.

"Yes, she's a good cook, and a nice lady, and as soon as you and I get the dishes done, you get to go home and test out your new bed."

"I want to stay here with Doris!" Sadie screeched.

Doris looked up and smiled. "Colt, one thing I learned from the Comanches was the way they raised their children. All the time I was there, I never saw an Indian child spanked or scolded or disciplined in any way. The toughest they ever got was when one of the women would look at a child and say, 'That, Sadie, is not the way the People act.' It worked. I've never seen such well behaved, or happier children in my life."

Colt looked at Sadie. "Sadie, that's not the way our people do things," he said calmly.

"Sorry, Daddy. Can I come back and visit tomorrow?"

"Yes, right after breakfast, if it's all right with Doris. Now let's do the dishes."

Doris tried to protest. He took her shoulders and sat her down in the kitchen. Then Colt and Sadie washed the dishes and cleaned up the table and the rest of the kitchen.

"Could I arrange for you to come in every day and do my dishes?" Doris asked.

He snapped a dishcloth at her, barely missing.

They left soon after that. He explained he had an early training march tomorrow. Sadie hugged Doris and then Danny and they walked back to their quarters.

"I really like Doris," Sadie said as she held her father's big hand. "I wish so much that she was my new mother." She looked up at her father but he stared straight ahead.

"We'll see," he said, thinking already about the training for tomorrow.

At six A.M. the Lightning troop was assembled in front of the Fort Commander's office. He came out precisely on time, stepped into his saddle on the black he always rode, and told Lieutenant Petroff to lead the troops out due west.

When they were a mile away from the fort, he called Petroff to his side.

"Today, we'll ride out ten miles at top speed, then find a dry place without any water and work on tracking and knife fighting. We have ten Tonkawa scouts along today. Each one will take two men and train them for two hours. The other twenty-five men will be given a tracking assignment. They have to find you after you ride away two miles.

"Two men will be trackers, the other eighteen following. When the first two men find you, assign two new ones as the trackers and ride away two miles in a circle around our knife fighting position. Continue until all men have tracked, or you've been gone two hours. Then return to the knife fight area.

"Oh, the Tonks have been instructed to get rougher this time. Both parties will be using lath stakes, a foot long instead of real knives. All will have blunt ends. The Tonks will bring blood on every man. Not kill him or disfigure or break any bones, but each man will be blooded before the knife fighting is over."

"Isn't that a little rough, sir?"

"Not as rough as being killed by an Indian knife on a real patrol fight. We'll see what you decide. You're the first man to be trained, and the first blooded. I'm second."

Then they rode, alternately cantering and galloping to cover the ground faster.

At the dry site the entire company gathered around as Major Hardng gave them the word.

"This is level two. Put your man down with a death blow and the match is over. If you can't do the job, learn every trick the other man uses until you can do it. Let's go."

Hatchet grinned as he faced Lieutenant Petroff. The older Petroff had been in his share of knife fights, and could handle a blade. He used the lath well, almost gained a killing throat slash but

Hatchet jumped back and slashed at the officer's left arm. The rough lath scraped off skin and blood showed. Then in a lightning fast series of thrusts, fakes and body contact moves, Hatchet tripped Petroff, fell on his chest trapping his knife hand at his side and pushed the lath against the officer's throat.

"You dead!" Hatchet cried and everyone cheered.

Petroff got up, an embarrassed look on his face. "That was good work," he said to Hatchet. "Congratulations." He held out his hand to the smaller Indian who laughed and caught the hand in the white man's gesture. Before Hatchet knew what happened, Petroff had gripped his hand, pulled him forward and swept his feet out from under him and fell on Hatchet. Now, Petroff's issue fighting knife was across Hatchet's throat.

"You dead, too!" Petroff said, and again everyone cheered.

Hatchet got up, his anger showing on his face. Petroff put his hand on the Indians' shoulder.

"Hatchet. No anger. I'm leader. Leader must win to keep honor with troops. You're the best man with a knife I've ever seen. I tricked you."

Hatchet grinned and looked at his next victim, Major Harding. The Indain won with a quick thrust into the Major's midsection less than thirty seconds after the lesson began. Major Harding saluted Hatchet, clapped him on the back and sent in the next man.

The knife training finished before the trackers came back. The men worked on what they had learned among themselves. Colt told them that the next phase of the knife fighting would involve each man facing another member of the company. Those who won their fights would be through. The losers would be teamed to fight each other, until there was only one man in the company who did not win a knife fight. He could chose any other man to fight, and would have to fight until he won.

When the first tinges of darkness streaked the plains, Major Harding fired two shots with his pistol, and the trackers came galloping back to the site.

They rode in the dark to the first small stream, dismounted and set about cooking their meal of the day. They had been issued salt pork and beans and hardtack. The beans had been cooked the night before, and now had to be refried along with the salt pork. It made a filling meal with the hardtack. Large doses of strong coffee finished the meal.

They had a half hour to eat and get saddled up. Then the Lightning Company covered the eight miles to the fort in a little over an hour. The men spent another half hour rubbing down their mounts, watering them and feeding them. At last they could fall on their bunks and wonder if they really wanted to be in the Lightning Company.

14

After a week it had become a ritual with them. Every morning Sadie ran up the west side of the quad along the officer's quarters to Doris' rooms. She opened the door, waved at Major Harding who then went on about his business of running Fort Comfort.

Every noon and every evening, he went to Doris' quarters for dinner, and an evening of playing with the children and talking with Doris.

At first no one noticed. But when the same arrangement went into the second week, even the enlisted men began wondering what was going on.

Captain Riddle came in that morning, turned the chair around and sat on it so he could lean his chin on it's back.

"Things getting pretty thick between you and this sister-in-law widow of yours?"

"Huh? Doris? She's a great help with Sadie. Don't know what I'd do without her."

"That's obvious, Colt, what else?"

"What do you mean, what else?"

"The woman is taking care of your child all day. She's feeding you twice a day and you don't get home until after time for Sadie to be tucked into bed. The whole damn post is wondering about what's going on when the door's closed."

Colt jumped up, his face flushed, anger sudden and sharp tasted bitter in his mouth.

"What the hell . . ." he stopped as John puffed on his pipe and looked up at his friend through a curl of smoke.

"I'm not saying anything is going on, Colt. Just natural for the folks, and the women, to wonder." Captain Riddle knocked the ashes out of his pipe into an ashtray and began refilling the bowl. "Colt, seems to me you've found yourself a mighty good woman. She likes Sadie, she evidently can even put up with you. Why don't you just go ahead and marry her?"

Colt dropped down in the chair. "Asked myself the same question a dozen times a day, John. I don't know why. Maybe it's too quick. Milly hasn't been gone more than what? Five months. Don't seem decent somehow."

"Colt, not true. Milly would be the first to urge you to go ahead, you know that's true. She was level headed and honest, you told me so. She'd want you to be happy and to take care of Sadie, and at the same time take care of this nice lady who has nobody else."

Colt sighed. "Yeah, I guess you're right. But what if she won't have me?"

"If she won't have you, I don't know a damned thing about females. Like to lay a hundred dollar bet on that?"

Colt frowned, shook his head. "Might need the money for a honeymoon," he said and grinned.

They heard some commotion at the gate and looked out to see a pair of dispatch riders come in. Both walked their mounts over to the Commander's office. A moment later Sergeant Swenson brought in two identical dispatch pouches and gave them to Captain Riddle.

There was only one letter. Colonel Phil Sparkman would be visiting the post within two days on an inspection tour.

"Damn, why now?" Colt asked.

"Our turn, I guess," Captain Riddle said. "I better check on the masons and those blocks, and see if we can get the timbers up for the roof on that new section."

"Sergeant Swenson!" Colt called. The sergeant came in the door and waited.

"Lieutenant Petroff. Get him over here on the double. What time is it? Eight-thirty. Good." He drew out a fresh piece of lined paper and made some notes.

Captain Riddle went out and a few moments later Lieutenant Petroff came in.

"Major," he said, standing in front of the desk.

Colt gave him the paper. "Sparkman will be here in two days. He's damn interested in your company. I want you sharp and mean by Friday. Take your troops out today for target practice, prone twenty rounds each, and horseback under the neck, ten rounds each.

"Then work on hand to hand knife training. Start

the one-on-one combat with the winners sitting down, but the losers all go back to knife class then for the loser's round. Finish it off with an eight mile ride in an hour. That's all, Lieutenant."

"Thank you, sir," Petroff said. Saluted, didn't wait for a return and hurried out of the office.

The word was passed to all company commanders of the arrival of the Regimental and Department of Texas Commander. The whole pace of the fort picked up. Men moved quicker, jobs were done smartly, training was more precise, and retreat that night at sunset by the bugler was strictly observed, as every man outside stilled in his duties, turned and saluted the flag as it lowered.

Somehow the men sensed that this visit was something special. They had no inside information, they just felt that it was to be more than a regular inspection tour by their commander from San Antonio.

Doris heard the talk. She had been to a tea with the ladies of the post, and they all felt the anticipation of the colonel's visit.

Colt had given permission for all officers to bring their wives and families to the fort "at their earliest convenience." Four of the new officers indicated they would bring in their families.

That night at supper at Doris's quarters, they talked of nothing else.

"Why is he coming, Daddy?" Sadie asked.

"He wants to talk to us, see how things are. Commanders have to do that with the troops every so often."

"Keep us all on our toes?" Doris asked.

"Exactly."

Sadie was struggling with a piece of paper, and

Colt saw that she was working hard at making letters on it. She was learning her alphabet. He looked at Doris.

"She really is ready to learn," Doris said softly. "It's too bad we don't have a post school."

"If we get enough children here, we'll have to start one."

Danny rolled on a rug on the floor and squealed for attention. Colt picked him up and gave him a horse ride on his knee, then put him back down.

"That's a very lucky little boy down there, having you to take care of him, Doris."

"Thanks. We kind of need each other. I can help take the place of his parents, and he can take the place of my lost son."

Colt moved over next to her on the couch in the living room across from the fireplace. It was warm, snug, it felt like home.

"Doris, I feel the same way, lucky that you've been around when I've needed you to help out with Sadie, and feeding me every day."

"I love doing it, Colt Harding. You must know that."

"Shouldn't you be in some big town, looking over the crop, trying to find a rich husband?"

Doris laughed. "I gave up the idea of marrying a rich husband when I was thirteen. Right now I'm in no mood and in no position to chase off after a husband. I've done about all the looking I intend to do." She watched him a moment.

"Strange you should bring up the subject. The women today at tea were asking about the same thing in a roundabout way."

Colt took a deep breath. "Figures. Half the troops are wondering what goes on after dinner in here every evening."

"Let's not tell them," Doris said, an impish gleam in her eye. "Then they can invent all sorts of wild stories." She sobered at once. "Colt Harding. I told myself not to do this. I figured that you're a smart man and you'd guess what was happening. Maybe you have, maybe you haven't. So I decided it was past time for you and me to have a serious talk."

"I been thinking on it. Not the sort of thing a man rushes into."

"Rushing seemed slow when the Comanche were all around and chasing after us. I think you and me would work out just fine."

"You wouldn't mind a ready made family?"

"Land sakes, no! I love Sadie like she was my own. I did everything I could to help her those two months with the Comanche. I've known her a long time. And Danny, we'll I've known him since the first breath he took, and Will whacked him on his red little bare bottom."

"Then it's all right with you?"

"Say it Colt, you got to say the words."

Colt would rather face a Comanche. He took a deep breath and caught Doris' hand. "Doris Worthington, would you marry me?"

"Oh yes! Now kiss me before I start crying."

The kiss was short and gentle. She clutched his hand.

"When?"

"There's a preacher of sorts among the settlers, just downstream. He can do the marrying. After a month's engagement. Is that all right?"

"Of course. Whatever you want."

Sadie, who had been very quiet with her tracing, jumped up and ran into her father's arms.

"At last!" she said. "At last I'm going to have a new mommie!"

That evening they put Sadie down to take a nap and then settled on the couch watching the fire. He had his arm around her and she snuggled against him. Colt kissed her cheek and she turned to him and this time the kiss was long and he felt the hot flames of her mouth.

"Dear, sweet Colt. I've wanted you to kiss me that way since the second day on the trail. I just knew it would happen, that it would work out. I'm so happy, and warm, and full of good food. There for a while in the Comanche camp, I didn't think that I'd ever be happy again."

Colt kissed her and she leaned backward on the couch. He followed her and she moved his hand over one of her breasts.

"Darling Colt, just pet me a little and then kiss me once more and then you have to go. Tomorrow I'm going to make the announcement about our engagement to the ladies at the card game. It will be all over the post by noon."

Colt kissed her once more, his hand rubbing her breast through the cloth of her dress, then he lifted away, helped her stand and they walked arm in arm to the bedroom where Sadie slept peacefully.

"I really like having a family ready made," she said softly. "Of course, that doesn't mean we can't have a few more on our own."

Colonel Sparkman arrived at Fort Comfort a day late. The time was put to good use laying up the last of the adobe blocks and lifting poles across the new walls to act as rafters for the sheeting that would follow. Fifty new adobe blocks had been mixed with grass and tamped into the molds.

If it was dry enough the bricks could be removed from the molds in two days and then left to dry out thoroughly before being used on the fifty feet of the fort not yet built.

The colonel arrived with a delegation of only three other officers and a twelve-man guard and one pack horse for the colonel's tent and supplies.

He was put up in the best quarters on the post and his officers, not used to a long ride, settled down in the rest of the officer's quarters for a rest.

Colonel Sparkman sat in Colt Harding's office that morning an hour after he had arrived. He lifted a whiskey with branch water and toasted the fort.

"To the health of all your men, Major. In case you aren't sure why I'm here, it's to double check on your Lightning Company. Can you arrange a two day demonstration for me?"

"Yes sir. This afternoon we can show you how we train the men, and put on a shooting show and a demonstration of our horsemanship. We figure if we're fighting the plains Indains, we better be nearly as good on a horse as they are."

Colonel Sparkman smoothed back his dark hair and watched this young Pony Soldier major. Reminded him a lot of himself twenty years ago.

"Major. I'm looking forward to this. Needless to say, a lot depends on how well your men perform today. Now, let's get some early dinner and then move out with the troops."

"Sir, I'd like to make one suggestion. When we go out, I'd prefer to have you equipped the same way the men are. You can participate in the demonstration if you wish."

The colonel frowned for a moment, then smiled.

He gave a curt nod. "Good. I'd like that. Nothing I'd like better. About time I got my nose dirty for a change."

An hour and a half later Colonel Sparkman and Major Harding led the forty men of Lightning Company and one sergeant and one lieutenant two miles from the fort. They started off four men abreast cantering.

"This is our slow pace, Colonel Sparkman. We try never to walk our horses when we are going to a contact or on a chase. The canter is a natural gait for a horse and is not as tiring as a walk. We usually split our time fifty-fifty between a canter and a medium gallop.

Colt raised his hand, waited for the sergeants and squad leaders behind him to imitate the motion. Then he circled his closed fist and waved it forward.

"Gallop, sir," Colt said and the Lightning moved out at twice the canter speed. Colt held the gallop for a mile, then swung around into a dry ravine and came to a stop. They were in their regular patrol equipped form: light saddles, no saddlebags, boot for the rifle, scaled down material and rations, and one blanket.

"Sir, we travel light and fast. With this equipment we can do seventy-five miles in a day and have food ready for us at the end of the ride. We use from four to six Tonkawa scouts. Half of them are regular scouts, the other half are hunters, who use bow and arrow only to bring down game so we can live off the land, and avoid large scale provisions which would slow us. We never use wagons or carts or canon.

"Water is severely rationed. We always train in dry areas to promote the idea of on-the-march water conservation."

"Our first demonstration is horsemanship. Every cavalryman has been on foot. When he wished he was mounted again. Each of our men must pass this test before he can become a member of the Lightning Company."

Four men rode out thirty yards and tied their horses. They positioned themselves on foot five yards apart. Four men galloped their horses hard toward them, slowed just a little, snatched the men off the ground and onto the horse behind the saddle. The men returned to the spot, changed places and the men just picked up did the picking up.

"In a tough battle, sir, we figure we can save every man possible this way, even if he gets unhorsed or can't get to his mount."

"Can I try it?" Colonel Sparkman said. "Did you and Lieutenant Petroff have to pass this test?"

"Damn right, sir, we had to do everything the men do. And you're welcome to try." Colt said it grinning. "You're on the ground and I'll pick you up." They rode to the spot and Sparkman got down. Colt showed him what to do, how to hold up one hand to be caught and where to grab the saddle with the other hand, then bounce off his feet as he kept his hold and swing up.

"You might hit the dirt the first time, sir. We never try a man's first pickup at full speed. If you get in trouble, just let go and yell and I'll let go."

They went over it again, then Colt rode back twenty yards. He rode forward at just over a canter speed and held down his right hand. Sparkman grabbed his hand with his left, caught the saddle with his right, bounced on both boots and swung easily up behind the major.

Colt laughed with relief.

"Colonel, you were teasing me. You've done this pickup work before."

Colonel Sparkman laughed as they rode back to his horse. "Before is right, but not since I was eighteen and working a cattle ranch. Damn, but that felt good!"

The next demonstration was firing under the pony's neck.

"Which squad do you want to do this demonstration, Colonel?" Major Harding asked.

"Third Squad," the colonel said. Colt signaled to Petroff who called out squad three. They lined up fifty yards from the target, a pair of cardboard boxes used before. When they came past, Colonel Sparkman was amazed at how they hung by one stirrup, swung down and around the horse's neck and fired at the target.

He saw that out of the five rounds each man fired, there were at least two hits by each man.

Colonel Sparkman asked the squad to ride the other way, so he could get a look at them as an Indian might see them as they attacked.

"Amazing!" he said. "Absolutely amazing. They look as good as the Sioux I saw ride that way. You taught these men to do this in a month or two?"

"Yes, sir. But we have the best horsemen on the post in this company."

Four Tonkawa Indians appeared suddenly from one side, moving toward the troops where they stood with their mounts. The Tonks all had a foot long wooden lath to use for knives.

Four men from the company ran out to confront them, and the four individual battles were on. The fights lasted from thirty seconds to four minutes. Eventually the larger cavalrymen with the best skill won over their smaller opponents. But it was two wins for the Tonks, and two for the soldiers.

Colonel Sparkman smiled and reached for his canteen.

"Sorry, sir, no water," Major Harding said softly. "We all follow the same rules out here."

The colonel smiled. "Right you are."

For an hour Sparkman watched two men from the Lightning Company track two Tonks who had ridden off an hour before. Suddenly the company took rifle fire from the left. Every man dismounted on command, the wranglers grabbed five horses each and scrambled with them into a small low place away from the fighting, and the company spread out five yards apart taking whatever cover the men could find.

Rifle fire came again from the Tonks. Petroff had just moved one of his squads around in a flanking angle, when Major Harding fired two shots from his pistol ending the exercise. The Tonks came out of their cover holding their rifles over their heads with both hands.

Sparkman turned to Harding and shook his head. "Phil Sheridan isn't going to believe me. I've been telling him about what your men can do, have done. I've never seen such realistic training in thirty-five years in the army. Damn! I wish we could give every soldier in the army this kind of training, enlisted and officers. Think what we could do against the Indians then!"

"I agree, Colonel Sparkman. But as it is I have to lie to get enough ammunition for target practice."

Sparkman chuckled. "Seemed to me that you had a lot of fire fights with the hostiles. But I approved every report."

"Water break," Colt said to Petroff who passed the word.

Sparkman saw Colt take a drink from his canteen and he did the same. "One thing I can't figure out, Major. What in hell do you have left to show me tomorrow?"

"Plenty, Colonel." He looked at is watch. "Time we were moving back to the fort. Lieutenant Petroff. You may lead out. How far would you say we're from the fort?"

"A little over four miles, sir."

"You have a half hour to return this company to the fort gate. You may move them out whenever you wish. Your time starts now."

"Companннnnnnny!" Petroff bellowed. "Column of Fours. Form up on me!"

"Column of fours!" Sergeant Casemore shouted, rousting men off the ground and into the saddles. As the last man moved his horse into position, Petroff lifted his head.

"Forwaaaaaaaaaaaard Hoooooooooo!" They moved out at a canter and fifty yards later he lifted them into a gallop. They headed across the prairie toward Fort Comfort.

Colonel Sparkman and Major Harding rode to one side.

"Can he get us there in thirty minutes?" the colonel asked.

"Can and will. The man is a natural. Came out of the war with a field promotion, then cut back to sergeant. Next he went to West Point. Best man in my outfit."

"He must be if you've given him the Lightning Company."

They arrived at the fort in twenty-nine minutes

and thirty seconds.

"Well done, Petroff," Colonel Sparkman said.

"Thank you, sir. Do you wish to review the men?"

"I'd rather have a hot bath, Petroff. But you give them my congratulations." He turned and handed his mount to an orderly and walked carefully to his quarters. He knew he would be stiff in the morning.

Major Harding watched Colonel Sparkman walking away. He hadn't the heart to tell him about their ride tomorrow. He and the other officers would be at the major's quarters tonight for dinner. No wives. Doris had enlisted Ruth Kenny to help her with the meal.

Colt reminded himself this could not turn into a drinking bout. At least three of them had to be up early in the morning. He had planned a surprise fifty mile ride at lightning speed for the colonel. They would make an attack on a small bend in a creek exactly twenty-five miles out, then return. He hoped the colonel felt up to it.

The dinner was a smashing success. Colt took the occasion to announce his engagement to Doris to all who didn't already know. They toasted the bride. Two hours after the dinner and cigars, Colt broke up the session.

He had taken Colonel Sparkman aside before he made the move.

"Thought I should warn you, Colonel. We're going on a fifty mile ride tomorrow. We'll go out twenty-five at attack speed and launch a fire fight against a nasty bend in a small creek. When we defeat the creek, we'll take a five minute medical break, then return at speed."

"Fifty miles?"

"We'll leave at five A.M. and return about four

P.M. That allows an hour for the fire fight. We'll make the trip with one canteen of water per man and no rations."

"Christ! You trying to kill these men?" Then he chuckled. "And you have a waiting list to get in this outfit?"

"True. Ten troopers have passed the riding and shooting tests and are waiting for openings."

"Phil Sheridan will never believe me. I've got to go along. I might regret it for a week or so, but the dispatch I'll write Sheridan will be a beauty."

15

The Lightning Company men were not surprised when they received double servings for breakfast at the mess hall that morning.

"We're gonna catch hell today," one trooper said.

"Show off for the old man colonel is what it is," another said.

"Yeah, but did you see him do that pickup yesterday? The Old Man is a regular guy in my book."

Lightning troop had been roused out of bed at four A.M. had breakfast and ordered to saddle up and get ready to move out at five.

Colonel Sparkman stood at the Fort Commander's door waiting at five minutes until five. He rode around the parade grounds, letting his horse walk, getting the feel of her. It had been a long time. Fifty miles. He chuckled softly. How did he get into these situations?

It would take six strong men and a half-inch chain to keep him off this ride. The troops came into line. Sparkman liked this young up-from-the ranks lieutenant. He was going to get his promotion damned fast, ahead of schedule.

The company fell in to Casemore's barking command and the lieutenant took a report. He sat waiting and ready for his commander. It was still a minute until five. At precisely five o'clock, Major Harding came out and took the morning report from the lieutenant. He looked over at Sparkman and saluted.

The colonel saluted in return and trotted over to join him.

"Major, let's go for a ride and have a picnic!"

They were off.

After the first hour they had covered seven miles. The Lightning Company men were settling into a groove, adjusting to the pace, joking as they rode along.

Up front Harding rode spur to spur with Sparkman. The older man was starting to look tired, but he would never even hint at it. He reached for his canteen, then pushed his hand away.

"I saw Phil Sheridan in St. Louis two weeks ago. He asked me about your Lightning Company. That's why I'm here. He told me to watch you in action if I could, demonstration action, not combat with the Comanche. He's interested. Your ideas tie in with some plans he has of his own."

"Colonel, I figured I had to do something. I'm tired to death of reacting to the savages. That way they have the advantage. Like the way they tried to raid our paddock. We staved them off, but we were lucky. The Lightning Company fell out in seven minutes, ready to ride and we took off after them. We probed and rattled them and in the end, we caught them because we could ride faster than they could drive two hundred horses."

"Without Lightning you're telling me you could have lost two hundred head of horses?"

"I'd say most of them. They scattered a few. But if I had taken out a regular company that night it would have cost us half an hour to forty-five minutes to get in the saddle. By that time we probably would never have caught them."

Colt sent a long look at his colonel.

"Damnit, Colt! Stop looking at me that way. I'm not about to drop out of the saddle. And don't you dare call a rest stop or do anything that you wouldn't normally do on a training run like this. If I can't keep up, I'll track you and find you at the bend in the creek. But I warn you, I'm a tenacious old son-of-a-bitch. Once I get my teeth into something I don't let loose without one hell of a battle."

Colt laughed and so did Sparkman.

Colt lifted the troop out of canter and into a paced gallop as they sped across the miles.

Two Indians showed up on their left flank and Sparkman pointed to them. "Trouble?"

"Tonks. Just letting me know they're still there, doing some outriding for us."

"Good. How long before we can train some of our own cavalry men to do the job your Tonks do?"

"Never. They are better than our own men could ever learn how to be. They have twenty-thirty years of training in tracking, riding, hunting. Besides, they know the territory. I think the Army is right in that aspect. We should continue to use local Indians as scouts whenever possible."

They rode three hours without stopping, and at the end of that time Colt determined that they had covered a little over twenty miles.

They took a short break and let the mounts drink and stand splay footed a while to rest. The men were given the word they could drink out of the small creek above the horses. Nature was served as well, and fifteen minutes later they were back in the saddles moving forward.

As they came up on the creek, Petroff sent out a six man scouting patrol. They returned saying there were at least fifty hostiles holed up in the bend of the creek. There was little cover besides the creek bank, about a four foot cut in the plains.

Petroff split his forces, sending two squads in at forty-five degree angles to the creek bed for a crossfire. Colt and the colonel watched from their mounts as the men moved up, then left their horses and worked their way through the brown grass to within a hundred yards of the creek bend.

When all squads signalled by hand that they were in position, Petroff triggered his pistol twice quickly to give the order to fire.

Each man had been told he would have twenty rounds to blast from this position. When the rounds were expelled, the men worked forward again, crawling through the grass.

"If the Indians can't see us, they can't shoot us with lead or arrows," Colt said. "If they use hit and run, we can too. If they are masters at slipping off into the plains or the woods and vanishing, then we must be, too."

"Fight the Indian with his own tactics," Colonel Sparkman said, as he thought about it.

"Right. We can't use the mass attack ideas that

won for us in the Civil War. It isn't practical, it isn't possible against the Indians, because you never have a fixed target. That's what I want to change. I want to go after the Indians in their camps. That's the only way we'll ever convince them to come into reasonable reservations and stop them from killing civilians."

They watched then as the men fixed their bayonets and charged the river bank. Petroff called for half the horses to be brought up. Half the troop mounted and raced after him into the plains to the east of the river bank. He spread them into a twenty man front and they charged firing their pistols as they drove forward.

Twenty minutes later the attack was over and Lieutenant Petroff came back and reported his losses.

"Sir, we have had six men killed and twelve wounded. The enemy loss figures at twelve killed and at least a half dozen wounded who were seen being helped away. The dead Comanches have been made certain of, and four rifles recaptured along with eight pistols. The bows and arrows have been broken and the arrow points kept to be discarded on the ride to the fort."

"Report noted and we offer our congratulations."

As the exercise finished, four Tonkawa Indians came into the area. They carried twenty grouse and pheasants over their shoulders. One Tonk built a fire, gathered wood, and dug a shallow ditch beside the fire.

Two of the Indians found clay they wanted, cut off the bird's feet and heads and then coated the bird, feather and all with the thick, red clay. When the fire had burned down to coals, a layer of the coals was dragged into the ditch. Then the birds were put in side by side, and more coals and dirt were dragged around the birds until they were covered.

The same Tonkawa "oven" was dug on each side of the main fire and birds put in to roast. Then the fire was built higher over the birds, but not enough to create too much heat.

A half hour later the meat was cooked. The Tonks dug out the birds, broke off the hardened clay that pulled off the pheasant's feathers and skin and left a roasted bird for the eating.

There were no mess kits or forks. The men shared the birds, pulling the steaming meat apart with their hands. Each man had half a bird.

The colonel got one to himself, and Colt and Petroff shared another.

"Never seen that done before," Sparkman said. "How does it taste, Colonel?"

"Damn good. I'd guess this is a sample of what your Tonks can do to provide food for the troop on a three or four week jaunt. I never saw a bird as we came through this morning. On a forested place you'd have venison?"

"Quite often. A company-sized group like this can eat up a small buck or a full sized doe in one meal. Nothing to carry. On a long march, we do take knife, fork, cup, coffee, salt and one tin plate per man."

"All the comforts of home," Sparkman said laughing.

He ate half the bird, then took the rest to Sergeant Swenson who came along as the major's orderly.

"Sergeant Swenson," Colonel Sparkman said. "Has he been with you for a long time?"

"In two different posts. He's good at his work. I'll take him with me wherever I go, if he wants to come.

I'd say the same for Lieutenant Petroff if I could swing it."

He turned to Petroff who had walked up after talking with Sergeant Casemore.

"Are the horses cooled down?"

"Yes, sir. Casemore say's he's ready."

"Ten minutes in formation."

"Yes, sir." Petroff went back to tell his top sergeant.

Petroff motioned to the major. "Colt, what time of year would you say is the best to attack the Indians, any tribe, anywhere?"

"No question at all," Colt said at once. "In their winter camps. The Indians reserves fall for hunting and making pemmican. Then winter is for surviving the cold and the snow. He isn't ready for a fight. He isn't off raiding or making war. Most Indians only raid and make war on whites or other Indians in the spring and summer."

Phil Sparkman laughed and slapped his thigh. "Damn, if I didn't know better I'd think you'd been reading some private letters I've been getting from Phil Sheridan.

"Remember this man is the Commander of the entire Military District of the Missouri. That's most of six states or territories, and that's where a lot of the hostile American Indians still ride free. I have a feeling he's moving up soon. It's going to be General Sheridan's job to put down the Indian uprisings and stop them from raiding the settlers who are constantly pushing west.

"In the whole district we have fourteen states and a million square miles to police, and only seventeen thousand cops. There must be two hundred thousand Indians scattered among ninety-eight different tribes we have to contend with."

"That's a mighty big order, Colonel."

"Damn big, Major. And I think Phil could use a man like you to help him get the job done in the Missouri District."

"Unlikely, Colonel Sparkman. He's a general, I'm just a brand new major trying to keep a frontier fort together." He signaled to Petroff who waved, and the men lifted into their saddles and formed a column of fours behind their officer.

They waited.

The colonel made it back to the base with no problems, where he inspected the troops, gave them a two minute talk about how great they were and took the liberty of giving them two free days with no drill and no duties. The troops cheered as they were dismissed by Lieutenant Petroff.

Sparkman rested in his quarters for the next two days. He took supper with Colt and Doris each night. On the last supper before he and his men were due to leave for Austin, Sparkman took Colt aside and spoke softly.

"Colt, I think I have a report that Phil Sheridan is going to eat up like gravy over a rabbit stew. He needs young men like you who can help train teams and companies who will be in the forefront of the Indian fights to come.

"I'm recommending that he transfer you to Fort Leavenworth in Kansas. It's not far from Kansas City, and it's Phil's headquarters for his fight against the Indians. A jumping off location."

"I don't know . . ."

"Course, Phil doesn't always take my advice. Usually he does. This isn't the kind of assignment that would be optional, Colt. If it comes it'll be an order."

"I know. A damn finicky mistress this Army is."

"True. I just wanted to give you an idea what's going on."

"Thanks, Colonel. I appreciate it."

A week later a wedding took place in the Major's quarters. Half of the post was inside and outside as the homesteader preacher did the honors and Doris cut the cake that Ruth Kenny made. There was a whiskey punch served in a big bowl but Captain Riddle made sure there was not enough to get anyone drunk.

The wedding took place on a Sunday afternoon and by three o'clock, Captain Riddle had shooed everyone out of the major's quarters. Ruth Kenny took Danny and Sadie for the night so the newlyweds could have their honeymoon night alone.

"This is going to be all of our honeymoon, I have a notion," Doris said. But she was smiling. She hadn't stopped smiling since the engagement had been announced.

When the door shut for the last time and Colt threw the bolt, Doris ran to him and fell into his arms and hugged him so tight he thought he was going to break.

"It's finally true!" Doris said. "I'm Mrs. Major Colt Harding. Just wonderful!"

Colt laughed. "You certainly are, for better for worse." He caught her hand and led her into the bedroom.

"Right now, before it gets dark?" she teased.

"Right now. Something I've been curious about, ever since I saw you put on that first tight dress up at Fort Brazos."

Doris giggled, and began to unbutton the snug fitting white wedding dress Mrs. Kenny had helped her make.

"You mean you think I'm hiding something else up here beside just me?"

"Are you?"

She stopped unbuttoning her bodice.

"Come look for yourself," she said.

Colt accepted, opened the rest of the buttons and spread the dress aside, then pawed through three more thicknesses of cloth and lace until her breasts stood firm and bare. They were full and had large round brown areolas and thumb-sized nipples that stood up erect and expectant.

"Lordy, lordy, lordy!" Colt breathed.

Doris sat on the bed and held out her arms to him, and again, Colt accepted her invitation.

It was two weeks later when a dispatch rider came into the fort and left his bags with Captain Riddle.

Colt had just signed the pomotion orders giving each Lightning squad a sergeant and a corporal. He made four more sergeants in other companies and leaned back smiling. He had the fort in the best shape it had been in.

A spate of hot fall weather had let them form up 400 more adobe blocks. There should be enough to finish the construction of at least the outside wall on the fort. The blocks would have to dry out first, which might not be until next summer. But it was a great start.

Captain Riddle came in with an odd expression on his face. He handed Colt two big envelopes. Each one was addressed:

"To be opened by no one but Major Colt Harding,

Fort Comfort, Texas."

In the upper left hand corner of the envelope was the scrawled signature that every officer knew: General Phil Sheridan.

"What the hell is going on?" Riddle asked.

"You're my adjutant—you're supposed to know," Colt said. His hand shook a little as he opened the first envelope. There were eight pages of writing. On top were orders transferring one Major Colt Harding to Fort Leavenworth, Kansas. "Where he will report to Colonel Ambrose Potter, Special adjutant to General Phil Sheridan, Commander Military District of the Missouri."

"Was this why Colonel Sparkman was here?"

"Seems to be. He said I might be taking a long trip. Seems I have some of the same ideas that General Sheridan does. The general wants me to be part of his "pacification" program for the Indians. Fort Leavenworth is his area headquarters for the push against the Indians."

"When do you leave?" Captain Riddle asked.

Colt looked at the orders again. "I have six weeks from the date on the orders to report. That would be . . . a month from today."

"Damn!"

Colt looked at the next page.

"Don't be such a grouch." He handed him the page. It promoted Captain Riddle to the position of Commander of Fort Comfort. He could request an additional two new officers for his new command.

"Damn, now I'm going to have to work for my pay," he said, but a smile belied his feigned disinterest.

Colt went through the rest of the orders. Mostly routine, but he was going. There was no question about that. No choice, as Sparkman said there might not be.

He opened the other envelope. It was the usual duplicate set of orders sent into the frontier. He gave one set to Captain Riddle to keep on file there.

Colt slapped him on the shoulder. "Well, Fort Commander, how does it feel to be in a major's T.O. slot for a change?"

"Scary."

"Why? You've been running the store here half the time anyway. Oh, you'll need a new clerk for your office. I'm going to take Sergeant Swenson with me as soon as I can. And if I can get Lieutenant Petroff assigned with me, I'll grab him, too."

"Then you'll need a new adjutant."

"Captain Kenny," Riddle said at once.

"Good choice." Colt stood. He looked around. He'd been here two years. It was going to be tough to leave. But the challenge of working close to or directly with General Sheridan gave him such a jolt he could hardly believe it.

He went to the door. "I better go tell the rest of the family that we're moving. What do you know about Fort Leavenworth?"

Sergeant Swenson said he'd like to go with the major when he could arrange it. Lieutenant Petroff listened a moment to Colt's suggestion and said he'd love to work with new "Lightning" kind of forces, to train them or lead them into battle.

Doris listened to the news quietly. Then she hugged him and kissed him.

"She is tough, isn't she, this mistress of yours? She crooks her finger and you jump and run halfway across the nation." Then Doris grinned. "But I have the advantage over her. She doesn't go to bed with you almost every night and I do. I think I'll be able to hold my own with her for your affection."

Sadie was delighted. "We get to go on a real stagecoach? What about a train? I want to ride a train."

"Possible, Sadie. But you must remember that our people are always polite and try their hardest to be nice to everyone."

"Yes, Daddy. I'll try."

Colt Harding looked at his family. Danny played on the floor beside Doris' feet. He was a lucky man. He had a family again, and a job that he could do better than anyone else. He wondered just how General Sheridan would use him. What would he let him do? Would he be out in the field most of the time? Would it be an office job? He'd hate that.

It would be field work, and some fighting. Winter was coming. This would be the ideal time to test out the General's views about attacking the hostiles in their winter camps.

Colt looked to the north. He couldn't wait to get there and get to work with General Sheridan.